White Week

And Other Stories

White Week

And Other Stories

Wojciech Chmielewski

Translated from Polish by Katarzyna Byłów

Revised by Mary R. Finnegan

Wiseblood Books 2025

CONTENTS

A PRAYER

A tram stops by Hala Mirowska. Those stepping off are mostly women—with just a few men among them. All the ladies smell lovely, fresh before work. Last night, a springtime storm passed over the city. Now, however, the weather is warm and dry. Lots of peonies in front of the marketplace building—stalls and stalls of them. Red and pink. Plenty of them this year, all poking their heads up, reaching towards the June sunshine. You can feel the sun already, though it is barely past eight o'clock. The scent of peonies gently mingles with that of the women passing by. Some women stop, buy a bunch of flowers. They will put them on their desks, by their computers, or give them to a friend celebrating her name day today. She will have brought eclair cake, poppy seed cake, or cheesecake with jelly on top.

A boy is selling strawberries. A t-shirt, shorts. Flip-flops on his bare feet, he is standing in the navy blue shadow cast by the building—*Polish strawberries, all freeesh . . . Polish strawberries, all freeesh*— he tries to lure the passers-by.

On the other side of the alley overflowing with peonies, four men are standing in a circle. They are all drunk, their faces flushed, exhausted. They are screaming at each other. They have been drinking since early morning, probably since five or six. They got their alcohol from the liquor store, which is open all night and has a separate entrance on the Hala Mirowska's ground floor.

Next, the passageway, where most stalls are already open. Right next to the entrance, there is an old lady with a kerchief wrapped around her head, nodding over a jar of chanterelles and holding a rosary. A young woman from the fish stand is looking towards the entrance to the market, towards the old lady sitting there. Her hair has been meticulously styled. She is waiting for someone.

Stall-keepers sprinkle water over vegetables and fruit using special water bottles. They have carefully arranged their fruit and vegetables, all fresh. The colors harmonise with the clear, early part of the day. Tomatoes of different varieties, some smaller, some larger, the tiniest are cherry tomatoes sold in plastic boxes. Kohlrabi and cauliflower, peaches from Morocco, citrus fruits arranged on a lining of soft paper. The whole picture is now arrested in swirling water droplets, illuminated by sun rays. The marketplace is quite busy at this time of the day—people keep arriving, asking if those strawberries have come from China. Some stalls have people queueing in front of them.

Next to the marketplace is a park, its benches covered by shade. The park is still empty, especially the playground and the hillock at its centre. You can slide down the hillock in a tin tube, straight into the sandpit. The morning air flows gently between the trees, and there is the scent of bark and soft swirls of city dust in the gaps between branches. A mounted police patrol moves along the main avenue of the park. A man and a woman, young. The horses' tails have been tucked, the animals prick their ears, their rumps shine. The hooves tap against the concrete paving blocks, slowly, majestically. The morning sun gleams on the woman's blonde hair, tied back in a ponytail, and on her breeches, the leather of her saddle, on her polished jackboots.

To the east of the park, an apartment building with its long arcades once again offers morning shade. It hosts stores and expensive restaurants, though they are still closed at this hour. People say it has the best sushi place in town. The pace here is always slower, and

I am hopeful that something might happen: that a person I have not seen for ages will turn up and we will sit down together for a while on the restaurant chairs, which are still stacked and chained together. Or perhaps an exchange with the girl who is now standing by the pedestrian crossing? She is wearing a black coat that reaches her knees, and when she starts walking, the coat's flaps open, showing flashes of her thighs in orange tights. The sun draws patterns on her legs.

The vast Grzybowski Square, now under construction, and the church at the end. Workers wandering between the pits. The construction site has been irregularly fenced off with crude wire, and passers-by are forced to walk along these newly mapped routes. An openwork labyrinth. The windows in the townhouses surrounding the square are lustreless. The morning light operates differently here because many of the windows have been boarded up with plywood and blackened wooden panels. No one has lived here for a long time—the city of the dead is right in the middle of this other city, the heart of the whole country. No one cares. The residents who are now walking across the square—each and every one of them, women, children, men—they are all going about their daily activities, illuminated by the light of a blooming day. And unless a piece of a brick falls from a crumbling townhouse and smashes on the pavement, nothing will disturb this springtime mid-week morning. Besides, even if something were to shatter in front of the elegant stiletto shoes of a lady now walking from the car park to her office—the one in neatly pressed trousers and a suit—she would just chitchat about it over coffee from the espresso machine in the marketing department of the company that employs her. Nothing more than a reason for her to be distressed, entitling her to the attention of many of her coworkers.

All Saints' Church is still and silent. Two massive towers, blackened at the top and capped with green spires, have always been here in this square, witnesses to a world which the people who rush past the wire fences know nothing about. And most likely, most of them never will. Anyway, no one knows for sure. Well, maybe only one or two people.

The church is bathed in the morning light, the stucco and the statues in the niches gleaming. There are wet stains on the steps of the staircase, the massive oakwood gates are unwelcoming, but the door in the arcade on the right is ajar. The anteroom is dark and chilly, there are holy images displayed on a blackened bench—Jesus in a manger, St. Joseph, St. Christopher, the Christ Pantocrator, Blessed Aniela Salawa, and some other postcards—all lit by a fluorescent light in a nearby display case. Just beyond the entrance to the side aisle stands Jesus teaching: a marble statue, his hand outstretched in a resolute, perhaps angry, gesture, though no anger can be seen on the Saviour's face. Just decisiveness and, above all, justice, as that is how we will all be judged one day, the hairs on our heads all numbered, the judgement inevitable.

Just opposite, in the chapel of Our Lady of Częstochowa, there glows a red light. Nearly invisible in the morning darkness under the great vaulted ceiling, it is obscured by a grille wrought with intricate floral garlands. But there it is, an eternal light. It glows—you must come closer. There are two kneelers. One is now used by a man in a railway uniform. Everything can be seen from up close, though the gates of the chapel are closed. He is kneeling down with his face in between the cast-iron flowers, which will leave a pink imprint on his cheek. The child points to his Mother's face with his tiny hand.

THE CHŁODNA STREET FANTASY

The eye meets the pavers for the first time. They are black, with a graphite sheen, evenly laid. They are smooth and warm, and when you put your open palm on them, you feel a slight vibration coming from somewhere in the direction of the fire station. It is the trams decelerating at the stop by Hala Mirowska. The setts paving Chłodna Street extend from the fire station to Towarowa Street. Your shoes can slip on the surface so you have to be careful, especially on a rainy day. Today, the June sun warms everything up: the treetops, the exterior of St. Charles Borromeo Church, the statues of saints in the niches, the yellow façades of long apartment buildings, and the red roof of the fire station. You can see the setts in many different ways, imagining, for instance, a city watched from above, with each sett being a house, a tenement, or an apartment block, and the gaps in between as streets. Such a world is infinitely larger than ours. Aside from the fact that it stretches from Elektoralna Street to Towarowa Street, and perhaps even further, it must be inhabited by beings superior in intelligence and more organized than a society of ordinary humans. Even though we tread on their rooftops, unaware of their existence, they are watching us all the time, well aware that neither passers-by, nor cars, nor trams can endanger them.

Special altars have been set up outdoors for a procession. At the first one, a passage from St. Matthew's Gospel about the Last Supper is being read. A woman standing near the altar is wearing a green linen dress, threads of the warp are clearly visible. She is large and her breasts droop towards the ground as she kneels down and then stands up, presenting her whole figure. The linen is slightly creased along her wide hips. She gazes up at the first altar where the procession has stopped. The altar stands out with its white and green, next to which the crowd seems colorless, and yet, there is so much color here today, including the red of the priestly chasubles. Petals spill onto the paving stones from baskets held by little girls dressed in white as the mystery of the transfiguration of wine and bread is now underway. It is time to kneel down. A priest walks, carrying the Blessed Sacrament down Chłodna Street, then towards Żelazna Street.

An afternoon in June. What might be happening in the underground city, in the metropolis made of setts arranged tightly together? The roofs of the houses are trampled on by the participants of the procession, snowed over by flower petals. Slowly, the procession makes its way towards the second altar. The altar boys walk in two rows, followed by women carrying a painting depicting the Most Sacred Heart of Jesus, followed by the church banners, each with attached ribbons held by girls dressed in blue satin dresses. The Blessed Sacrament is framed by the golden sun of a monstrance shrouded in a veil, travelling under a canopy carried by six men, three on each side, with two more men supporting the priest's arms. We keep walking through the city that is around us and upon the one that is under us.

The city down there is inhabited by snake-people. They are mysterious creatures and not much is known about them. One thing is certain: they are very different from the inhabitants of Chłodna Street and the surrounding area: Walicόw, Ogrodowa, Żelazna, Krochmalna, Grzybowska, or Wronia Streets. The existence and the secret lives of the snake-people must have been known to the

German writer Ernst Jünger, who as a young man was involved in witchcraft and demonology. He also experimented with drugs. He was famous for the bravado he displayed on the Western Front during the First World War and for his role in the occupation of Paris during the Second World War. In his journals, published as *Strahlungen*, he often expressed his fascination with snakes. For instance, on 26 July 1942 he wrote:

> In the night, I dreamed about a beautiful snake; its iridescent, steel-blue scales showed labyrinthine wrinkles like those on a cherry pit. The creature was so large that I could barely put my arms around its neck; I had to carry it a long way because no cage was available.

The snake-people are probably not happy when a crowd like this treads on the roofs of their homes. To them, it must sound like a hailstorm. In their own city, so different from ours, they gather in their houses to confer. The snake-people have a great advantage over us—they know we exist.

The second altar has been erected inside the gateway of a tenement at 20 Chłodna Street. It is the only building in this section, between Elektoralna Street and Żelazna Street, that has survived the carnage inflicted by the snake-people on the local population over seventy years ago.

The priest has placed the monstrance on a raised platform, and the people around kneel down. Now, they are standing up, spread across the street, wall to wall, with their faces turned in one direction. The afternoon sun illuminates bald heads, perms, fringes, and sideburns. Velour, cotton, nylon, linen, and wool, and, despite the summer heat, some women wear thin, colorful jumpers. My mother is not among them. She has never been fond of long ceremonies.

Since her illness, a recurring one that manifests in sudden attacks, she has had difficulty coordinating her movements. She can walk, but her gait is slow and unsteady. She decided to stay home and is now watching television for sure.

The excerpt we hear is about multiplying bread. "But where in this remote place can anyone get enough bread to feed them?" One side of the street is filled with fifteen-story apartment blocks, the other by a dirty-yellow structure spewed out by socialist realism and by a single surviving building at 20 Chłodna Street. Its façade bulges fancifully, and there is a broken clock right above the entrance. Has it been broken since the war? Religious pictures have been stuck on the windowpanes for the procession, some of them depicting our pope. " . . . About four thousand were present . . . After he had sent them away." We, too, are soon going to rise from our knees, but now we are singing: "From plague, famine, fire and war, save us, O Lord." The supplication is to protect the residents from the snake-people. Those who once inhabited the area experienced the snake-people's machinery of destruction, which had no mercy. Nothing but ruins were left here, the people shipped to extermination camps. All this as a punishment for constantly trampling on the sett city where these creatures lived. Jünger used to dream about them very often. He noted a certain general regularity of nature, incomprehensible and eternal, in their appearance and movements. On 12 July 1942, he wrote:

> Was with a woman in a shop that sold edible snakes. The merchant opened a drawer and, without looking, reached in and yanked out the creatures by the middle of their bodies. Before handing them over, he put miniature muzzles on them,

through which the little vipers' horns quivered. We paid twelve or fourteen marks for a medium-size specimen. Once I had awakened, I kept scratching my head over who the woman had been.

The procession moves on. Blind statues of cemetery children holding hourglasses in their hands bid us farewell; a scythe has been placed nearby, leaning against the wall. There are also broken cement floral garlands—the sad remains of the destruction wrought by the snake-people. They did not manage to raze the house at 20 Chłodna Street to the ground—its façade remains. They may have been in a hurry and forgot, or maybe it was something else. The clock most likely shows a specific time, but from the street the hands are not visible because the glass is dusty. The setts are underfoot, felt by everyone. Women in heeled shoes have to be careful not to step on the gaps between them. The heel can bend and fall off, and the women may twist their ankles. That is why we all walk slowly, to the rhythm of the song that surrounds us: "One bread that transforms into the body of Christ is born of many grains. One wine that transforms into the blood of Christ flows from many grapes."

There used to be a wooden bridge, here in this spot. When the snake-people invaded, the bridge connected two parts of the city, which was divided by Chłodna Street. The snake people crawled over Chłodna Street, in precisely the same places now walked on by the people in this procession. The city residents used the bridge back then to avoid deadly bites. No trace of it survives, except in the memory of some of those now walking behind the Blessed Sacrament. Maybe not even there. The majority of people, after all, have not experienced the machinations of those dwelling in the city down below, the one over which we are now walking; they do not know the snake-people, have never seen them, have never dreamt about them. But surely, there must be some people who do remember—some of those who are now walking, not looking at their feet, praying that the snake-people never again crawl out of their hiding places alongside Chłodna Street.

Ernst Jünger was fond of his dreams about snakes. Otherwise, why would he have devoted so much space to them in his diary?

> A restless, nervous night, triggered by air-raid sirens. Then I dreamed about snakes, particularly about dark, black ones that devoured the bright, colorful ones. I seldom get a feeling of terror from these creatures, which are so central to our dreams—for the most part, they seem to be showing me their side of life. Their fluid, swift, flexible character was described so beautifully by Friedrich Georg:

> And as the adder's belly
> Glistens silver,
> When quickly it flees, thus fled
> The garlanded brook.

> The primal force of these creatures lies in the fact that they embody life and death, as well as good and evil. At the same moment that man acquired the knowledge of good and evil from the serpent, he acquired death. The sight of a snake is thus an experience filled with incomparable dread for each of us—almost stronger than the sight of sexual organs, with which there is also a connection. (13 July 1943)

Beyond Żelazna Street, the buildings get chaotic and fractured, but the solemn procession, banners, and paintings make this part of Warsaw look a bit less ugly on this Corpus Christi Day. There is a leaning fence, behind which materials used for some unknown purpose have been stored for years, just opposite a dilapidated town-house at no. 25. Next to the fence is a completely ruined 27 Chłodna Street, a one-story townhouse with a protruding avant-corps. Who used to live here? People, none of whom have survived. The structure will soon collapse, and then the bulldozers will come. In the past, the townhouse probably had a yellow plaster façade, but today it is covered in mould, revealing broken bricks. The roof has collapsed. The townhouse is separated from the street by a crumbling wooden fence with a no-entry sign. On a warm June day, these dilapidated remnants are seen by crowds of festively dressed people. Why are they still here? After all, many decades have passed since the city has been destroyed by the snake-people. New residents have arrived, rebuilt what could be rebuilt, and settled in the neighborhood. It might be difficult to understand, but many women and men who are now walking down Chłodna Street know the answer to this question. It can be asked in a different way: who wants to have ruined houses in the city center? Perhaps the man wearing a white shirt and a formal suit jacket with wide lapels knows the answer? Or the one next to him, with a polo shirt tucked into his trousers, held up by a worn-out leather belt? A girl has tied her hair up in a ponytail and now her face is focused—she is praying. Her dress is gathered on her shoulders with an elastic band, the fabric has some of Poland's flowers printed on it: cornflowers and poppies. The girl is wearing sandals, and they touch the setts. The man next to her has such a huge head! And a flat face, and tiny blue eyes. Trousers made of gabardine, neatly ironed. My father has such trousers, maybe even two or three pairs, but they are now hanging in the wardrobe in the hallway, and one pair has been thrown over a chair in the dining room. He started drinking last night and, since today is Thursday and tomorrow is his day off, he will keep drinking till Sunday, or maybe longer, who knows. After he binges on liquor like that, he tends to sit on his bed holding his head in his hands and howling in pain. Maybe he sees the snake-people attacking our city again. There is no telling what he is up to.

In front of the tenement at 34 Chłodna Street, we all kneel. Another relic from before the invasion. Its façade is as flat as an ironing board. There are windows, balconies with rusted railings, some with ornaments—a lonely cube, still standing. Everyone can see that it once used to be crammed between other such tenements. Chłodna Street was a major avenue in the capital city with trams, restaurants, and stores, a bustling big-city life. Not what it is today. All that is left are the old tram tracks, where people are now walking, on which little girls are sprinkling flower petals.

An excerpt from the Gospel of Saint Luke. The road to Emmaus was certainly not paved: it was a rocky or sandy track, a beaten track, travelled by pedestrians and horsemen and donkeys loaded with goods. The travellers walked on and Jesus "himself came up and walked along with them." The people all around us are busy with their own affairs, just like those travellers were. They listen as the priest talks of breaking bread, then they will go back home and eat their bread—with lard, butter, margarine, plum jam, or with bacon. "Were not our hearts burning within us while he talked with us on the road and opened the Scriptures to us?" The hearts of people are now opening. This cannot be known by the silent witnesses—the sett-paved street, the dilapidated wartime remains. But the souls of those who once inhabited these townhouses, the surviving tenements and those which irrevocably turned into dust—they do know. They are here, circling around like sparrows looking for crumbs, sitting on rusted balconies, perched tightly on the transverse poles of church banners, perched on the canopy that shields the Blessed Sacrament. Souls only avoid contact with the setts. To them, the roofs of the snake-people houses are unclean and cursed.

The procession turns back towards St. Charles Borromeo Church. It is a great vantage point for looking onto Chłodna Street and the two church towers. Women pluck birch branches from the altar. The way back is slow, as if the procession takes an incredible effort, sacrifice, or challenge. Yet it is a simple walk along Chłodna Street, from the church to no. 34 and back. And the sun is shining today, and there is an early summer fragrance in it, the promise of hot summer days and holidays in just two weeks. Walking at a fast pace, an adult can cover this distance in about five minutes, it takes no more than a minute when riding a bicycle.

But something still vibrates in the air. The women keep looking up, but there is not a single cloud in the sky. Maybe the pressure is dropping, since people are beginning to feel sleepy. Ernst Jünger dreams about writhing snakes in occupied Paris:

> I began to feel better as I slept. I saw myself in a garden where I was saying farewell to Perpetua and our child. I had been digging there and my shovel opened a small hole in the earth, where I saw a dark snake napping. As we said goodbye, I mentioned this to Perpetua for fear that the child might get bitten by the creature while playing. Consequently, I turned around to kill it, but now I found that the garden harbored lots of snakes—knots of them were sunning themselves on the tiles of a derelict gazebo. There I saw dark red and blue ones, and others that were yellow, black and red, or marbled in black and ivory. When I started to fling them across the terrace with a stick, a bunch of them rose up and clung to me. I recognized that they were benign and was barely scared at all when I saw

our little boy beside me. He had followed me unnoticed. He picked them up by their midsections and carried them out into the garden as though it were all a jolly game. The dream cheered me up and I awoke invigorated. (4 September 1943)

I find the beauty of the snakes he described striking when compared to the people in the Corpus Christi procession. Have they no nobility, no grace, no allure? Obviously, they do, but I do not see it. Domestic images keep seeping into my mind: my half-conscious father and my mother, moronically click-clacking in her house shoes. They obscure the real picture of those who are walking by—the young ladies; and men, their torsos developed from playing volleyball and basketball; children with faces that know no fear of the black-and-yellow or any other kind of snake. These people are not afraid of snakes at all, and would not fear them even if they knew that they are now stepping on them, that Chłodna Street is a reptile city.

The procession passes by the exit to Waliców Street. From here, the church looks as if it were cast in silver. A tram used to go by, passing the church on the right and then along the tracks between the fire station buildings. Later, a glass link was built between the two buildings and the whole set-up broke down. Waliców Street has not been developed as far as Krochmalna Street. There are only pavements with parked cars, a dusty hedge, and trees standing where the destroyed tenements used to be. Let us pray for those who once lived here and looked out from their windows at a Corpus Christi procession and at the setts of Chłodna Street, dry in the summer, glistening after the rain, with wastewater flowing along the street on both sides, down the gutter. Let us pray, since they will never again walk down Chłodna Street, nor Waliców Street. And the snake-people?

Will they return? Who knows? Waiting, curled up, basking their bodies in the sun. Perhaps they are preparing some new hell for those walking these streets, like the woman who has just tripped on the curb but kept her balance with the help of another woman. That one will be punished for her immediate assistance, too. The eye of the snake is forever open, and it sees everything. It mercilessly records every human weakness, every single inkling of compassion.

Beyond Waliców Street, there is an apartment block at 11 Chłodna Street with a grocery shop opening onto the road. Several people have already lined up along it because the spot provides a clear view of the stairs leading up to the church. That is where the fourth altar has been erected.

The canopy is already folded, superfluous. The priest has approached the altar and is now setting the golden sun of the monstrance on it. Suddenly, St. Charles Borromeo Church becomes a hill, and all those kneeling down around it become as wanderers on their way to the top. People recall Jesus's prayer: "that they may be brought to complete unity. Then the world will know that You sent me and have loved them even as You have loved me." Perhaps the people around the altar are already one body in a city that will never give them away or betray them.

At this very moment, two tall trees—two aspens growing on either side of the church—start to tremble. Their leaves send flashes of reflected sunlight that gleam upon the people, and though the sun's power is waning, they still stare into the trembling leaves in silence and try to read the meaning of this sign coming from the trees. The roots of both of these trees reach deep down, beneath the layer of setts, to the very center of the reptile city. Since the trees are giving us signals by moving their crowns, there must be something going on there right now, and that never bodes well for this city. The aspens stand in opposition to the snakes, and they risk a lot because their roots can easily be attacked and destroyed if someone were to inform on them. What do these fluttering leaves mean? At worst, we will be facing another war; at best, the snake-people are just unhappy about this vast congregation of people walking over the roofs of their houses—they are a nuisance. In such cases, there may be retaliation and further warnings, such as a gas explosion in a flat at 11 Chłodna Street, which the firefighters from the fire station will have to put out.

The priest at the altar has noticed the signals but does not react. He continues preaching that we should eat the body and blood of Christ as often as possible, only then are we in communion with Him and only then are we one with Him. We can then effectively defend ourselves against the forces of evil, against the darkness that invades from everywhere, through Holy Communion these forces lose access to our hearts. But—here the priest points at those of us who are standing around—since we have come here today, this is clearly what we wish to achieve, so we have nothing to fear.

Finally, gazing at the trembling crown of an aspen tree, he quotes the following words of our Savior: "I saw Satan fall like lightning from heaven. I have given you authority to trample on snakes and scorpions and to overcome all the power of the enemy; nothing will harm you. However, do not rejoice that the spirits submit to you, but rejoice that your names are written in heaven." Amen.

Amen. He has finished and the feast is over. People are slowly dispersing. Some go towards Ogrodowa Street and Biała Street, others go in the opposite direction—to Krochmalna, Ciepła, and Grzybowska Streets, and the rest return to Żelazna Street and Wronia

Street. Colorful petals are strewn on the setts paving Chłodna Street and the superfluous tram tracks stuck among them. I stand on the rooftops of the reptile city. I do not want to go home. Jesus walked down this street with us today, but now he has taken refuge in the church. I am alone.

GERTRUD VON LE FORT

She takes a seat on a chair set up on the terrace and looks at the mountains. Fall. The peaks snow-capped, as always, the valleys in green and yellow. Gertrud is looking at the silhouettes of the peaks, dark against the sky in the evening light. Oberstdorf is profoundly quiet at this time of day. Behind Gertrud, there is a spacious living room and several logs are burning in the fireplace. Gertrud wraps her blanket more tightly around her knees. She is alone and the sun is charting the last stains of colour on a snow cap.

Today Gertrud wrote ten pages of her new novel then dictated letters to her secretary, and then after the lady left, she ate a light meal consisting of a slice of dark bread, some sheep's cheese, and an apple. It would be nice to celebrate the end of such a glorious day. A glass of red wine would be the apex of the evening, with the peaks now quite black and a deep shadow cast across the valley. Gertrud, however, does not move from her chair. She is not thinking about anything—the writing, meetings with her readers, with her publisher, conversations with her closest friends, a cup of coffee at a table in the garden of the patisserie on the Residenzstrasse in Munich, or the Asamkirche, where a golden skeleton is grinning its teeth; none of that occupies her mind as she is sitting on the terrace of her house. After all, here, in this mountain resort, she has found peace—at last, she can write. Her German readers retrieved her after the war, after all that the nation has done to itself. They cherish, they read, they write letters. Gertrud is working, day after day—that is how life is fulfilled—and the alpine air serves her well as she sits down at her desk each morning.

Around the same time, a few hundred kilometres northeast of Oberstdorf, in Warsaw, Mania has lost her job at the hostel of the State Motor Transport company at the West Railway Station. The reason: during working hours, Mania had gone out with some guys to the station bar to drink vodka. She was dressed in a maid's outfit with apron, striped blouse, a short black tie. An ordinary girl from the village of Opacz, who got herself a job at a major railway station. Because it is big, with trains and buses, crowds of people pass through the dirty station passageway every day. Under the peeling paint of the ceiling, a cold, mortuary-like light shines on them, whether they are aware of it or not, and they keep going about their business, thinking about the hours ahead, tormented by their morning hunger, so they buy rolls, sweet rolls, and on Fridays, smoked meat sandwiches.

It is not quite eight o'clock, yet Mr. Józio is already carrying a pint of beer across the station hall. People who are rushing to work look at him—he looks unassuming, unshaven, there is hair sticking out of his face. He blends in well with the overall station background, which is why the girls from the Academy of Special Education do not notice him at all. Mr. Józio is a sort of urine stain that has to be avoided, the unpleasant smell that is noticeable in the passageway on a daily basis, making it difficult to eat the first sandwich and drink the morning coffee.

Mr. Józio certainly knows Mania very well. He lives in a tiny house by the railway tracks and has no electricity, since it has been cut off. It is cold as hell there, so he spends most of the day at the station, just like Mania. Perhaps she was in love with the guy who persuaded her to skip work back then, the guy with whom she wanted to have a drink; perhaps she thought that when she came back from her prolonged break, everything would somehow be fine. Then again, she had probably drunk alcohol at the hostel before, more than once, for there has always been drinking there. But this time, she really got on the wrong side of someone. Before she turned into a stinking station monstrosity with a frostbitten face, she may have been a cool girl, with a satisfying sex life in one of the hostel rooms. She may have been used by executives, and later maybe even by intercity bus drivers, who knows. One thing is certain: As she was indulging in a drinking spree during her working hours someone spotted and reported her, and she was fired by the then-director.

Gertrud used to travel a lot. She attended readings all over Germany, Switzerland, France. She attended author meetings, gave lectures, visited cathedrals, monasteries, and art galleries, and caught up with friends. During her travels she had once met a Jewish woman, Edith Stein, who had converted to Catholicism and was about to become a Carmelite. Edith wore her dark hair parted in the middle and was familiar with Gertrud's books, though Gertrud sensed something else in her, perhaps a force that made her ponder the woman's fate, especially at a time when Barkilphedro and his men had just taken power in the country. The women exchanged letters afterwards. "Dear Honourable Lady" was the title with which Edith addressed Gertrud, after the former had donned the monastic veil. Her letters arrived from a convent in Echt, near Cologne, and Gertrud kept writing back. She later read Edith's letters many times over, including on the veranda of the house in Oberstdorf, but especially after Barkilphedro had murdered Edith and her sister Rose in Auschwitz. For example, the following passage:

You will always find a family home with us. Trusting that our peace and silence will radiate out into the world, helping those who are still on pilgrimage, always reassures me; especially when I think that I have been called to this miraculous hiding place before many worthier than me. You cannot imagine how immensely it embarrasses me when someone speaks of our "life of sacrifice." I have lived a life of sacrifice in the world. Now, almost all the burden has been taken away from me, and in this fullness I have everything that I did not have before. There are sisters with us, of course, from whom the Lord requires daily sacrifice. And for me—I expect—there will be a time when the call to the Cross becomes painful; now the Lord is still treating me as a little child. For now, let us unite spiritually, let you, should you feel the need to take a breath— at least in this way—find shelter among us, and God willing, one day it will actually happen.

Mania was also sacked because many people had seen her drinking at that particular time. Had she simply drunk two shots and gone back to work, no one would have minded. But she did something else. Someone pushed her, maybe she had a drunken brawl with the guy who was supposed to be hers and then he pushed her and then she flew into the glass display case that to this day mars the appearance of the filthy passageway—though it is nearly impossible to make it worse as everything is distorted here, even the people momentarily entering this abyss—that is to say, the underground— the everyday commuters hurrying to work. Anyway, Mania's back slammed against the big glass panel, there was a clang, and hundreds of glass shards fell on the grimy floor. There was a commotion; people gathered. When it comes to something like that, it is easy to get reported. Here she was, a drunken Intercity Bus Transport hostel worker lying among glass shards on the floor, unable to stand up.

People were laughing, and her guy probably reflected that there was no point in going on with it all. It was nonsense after all, and he hadn't helped her up. He must have been drunk too.

Mr. Józio, on the other hand, is a supplier. He supplies the owner of a stall, a fat woman who sells beer without a licence (no one holds a licence here, as long as the area belongs to the Intercity Bus Transport company, there will be beer for sale), bringing her plastic bags filled with vegetables that he has collected from a dumpster at the Hala Kopińska marketplace. It is not that far away, and it is worth it for him. The woman takes out a cabbage head, a few carrots, cauliflower, two onions—darn, these are already running—she puts the onions back in the bag.

"And how much do you want for it?"

"A can of beer."

The woman brings him a bottle of Cossack, but before she does, Mr. Józio dumps the rest of the vegetables along with the plastic bag right over the fence, onto the railway tracks, which may also be the Intercity Bus Transport company's land. Nobody knows, nobody can tell. He then greedily drinks his beer at a table set up in front of the stall. It takes him less than a minute. He walks off and is on his way.

Gertrud closes the door to the veranda; she is now in the living room downstairs. On a shelf above the fireplace there is a glass ball, a souvenir from Venice. There is also a Piranesi engraving, hanging on the wall opposite the window, depicting the fountain in front of the church of Santa Maria sopra Minerva in Rome. The room is filled with heavy furniture—couch, chairs, a desk—and the oak floorboards reflect their shapes. A lamp has been lit. It is very quiet. Gertrud von le Fort walks up the stairs, her wrinkled hand tightly gripping the railing.

After she was fired for drinking, Mania quickly found a new job—she became the manager of the station's toilets, located at the end of the filthy passageway. Such spots are often centers of social life at railway stations. Different people come to Mania, and she has drinks with them. The parties last for hours, with a steady rotation of attendees. How many years has she been a resident toilet lady? Hard to say, five, eight, twelve. Sometimes she reads books, because times have changed and some people bring books from their home collections to sell for peanuts at the station. Mania found one story especially memorable, a story of a girl named Veronica and her grandmother, as well as her aunt Edelgard, all living in Rome. Mania wrapped the book in grey paper and kept it in a drawer in her desk in her "office" in the toilets. She found the descriptions of the city particularly appealing. She could imagine herself exploring Rome's churches and the ruins of the ancient world along with the book's protagonists. How sweet the fragrance of flowers and herbs on the slopes of the Gianicolo! She sympathised with Edelgard's sudden loss of faith, her breakdown, her despair. After all, the aunt had cared so lovingly for little Veronica, had nurtured her. Why had her prayers not been answered? In the house where the three women lived together, the grandmother surrounded herself with works of art, portions of the great heritage of antiquity. She supplemented her love of antiquities with a Renaissance bust, a Baroque miniature. And flowers everywhere. Every day, Aunt Edelgard brought fresh flowers from Campo di Fiori and arranged them in crystal vases that reflected the morning sun shining over Rome. The fountain in front of the Santa Maria sopra Minerva features a statue of an elephant. Why had nothing like this ever happened to Mania, why had she never seen this elephant, why was she sitting in the loo wiping up drunkards' puke? She was drinking more and more herself. Once, after binging on vodka, she tore up the novel about Veronica and threw the shreds into the filthy toilet. She flushed it.

Mr. Józio is walking down the station hall, gently carrying a beer-filled tankard in one hand and a clear plastic bag in the other. His filthy head is topped with a black leather cap. It is not clear where he is going. Probably not to his flat in the railway building, as the electricity and heating there have long since been turned off. To fall asleep, he needs to be properly anaesthetised. Then, if he lies in bed in his winter coat and piles torn quilts up over himself, he may be able to endure the night. At dawn, he goes straight back to the railway station to warm up his old bones, and the people there are nice too. Travellers always leave something behind—you just have to look for it, rummage around, look in all the nooks and crannies, and Mr. Józio knows these by heart. He passes by a souvenir shop where clay angels look at him from behind the glass. Mr. Józio used to have a very good job—he was a shunter and worked for the railways, in Szczęśliwice or Odolany, but once the bosses caught the whole group—including the drivers—drinking vodka. And this at the time when the railways were laying people off on a massive scale. They sacked them all, and soon a large group of them were employed by another company, but somehow, they failed to involve Mr. Józio in the deal, for which he holds a grudge to this day, still choking with resentment. After all, they keep seeing each other, as those other railway workers enjoy a pint of beer in the bar at the West Station. Sometimes they even drink something stronger, furtively, under the table.

Gertrud von le Fort, the author of the novel treated so harshly by Mania, titled *The Veil of Veronica*, is now preparing to go to sleep.

As she closes the window curtains, a strong gust hits the panes. The wooden shutters creak. Gertrud slowly removes her clothes, which she hangs neatly on the chair, without a single fold. Then she puts on a nightdress trimmed with lace and slips under the duvet. The bedroom is illuminated by a single lamp on the night table. It is quiet in Oberstdorf. The spruce trees are shivering on the slopes, winter is slowly approaching. Before she falls asleep, Gertrud sits down comfortably, a large cushion behind her back. She ponders the pages she has written today, whether they are good or true, whether the story is coming together. It does seem to be coming together nicely, but there are still seventy pages to go, and her publisher in Munich keeps urging her on, impatiently waiting for the book.

Then Gertrud recalls her mother, a good, proud woman. After her father's death, her mother isolated herself with the children in Ludwigslust, where she taught them everything—songs, painting, knitting. They read Tolstoy and Balzac. There were long hours of silence, of working in silence. Gertrud wrote poems. And then her mother took them to Rome and the young girl saw an elephant in front of the Santa Maria sopra Minerva for the first time. On the other side of the square, there was the Pantheon, all dark. It was a very long time ago, in another world. Flocks of pigeons were circling over Rome as the capital of the world faced the bright blue sky.

A practised movement of the aged hand. From the table drawer, Gertrud takes out a rosary she keeps in a tortoiseshell box, a gift from the Holy Father. The beads rustle, the woman begins to pray. The wind in Oberstdorf has gone to sleep for good.

Mania makes her bed of old cardboard boxes. Behind the railway station, in the direction of Pruszków, on the right side of the tracks, there is a traction pole. The homeless have made a camp underneath it. Black silhouettes appear and disappear around Mania's bed. They stagger around. There are voices that Mania hears as a steady hum. She pays no attention to the noisy long distance and local trains. She is not cold. Since she has been spending nights in the passenger waiting rooms, and up on the platforms in winter, her face is frostbitten, puffy. She is used to the cold. She covers herself with a frayed quilt she retrieved from the garbage. She feels good, strange, since she has not been drinking, despite those dark men toddling around her bed offering her methylated spirits, diluted with water, from a plastic bottle. Even her leg does not hurt today, though it is covered in festering wounds and wrapped in dirty bandages. In the event of necrosis, doctors will have to slash it off. Some kind strangers had taken Mania to the hospital on Barska Street because of her leg, but she ran away back to the station two days later. She will see how it goes. Mania does not pray. Before going to sleep, she only repeats a phrase her grandmother once taught her: *Oh, Mother of love, sorrow and mercy, pray for us.*

THE ROMA WOMAN

Martin was doing his weekly shopping at the local farmer's market. He filled his basket with potatoes, bananas, and tomatoes he handpicked from the stall. He also bought cleaning supplies from a man running his shop out of the back of his truck—two litres of the green, general-purpose Ludwik in plastic bottles.

The dirty sky cast reflections on the people swarming among the tents and stalls. The biggest queues were, as always, at the bread and meat sellers, who served people from high up in their meat vans. Hands stretched out from the throng, grabbing cuts of pork belly, sausages, potatoes, and offal. On the platform, money was counted. The woman vendor drank coffee from a transparent cup.

Two Roma women were positioned at the entrance to the market, selling blouses. They came every week, but today there was also a girl, several years old, hanging around them. The girl would run through the muddy market aisles, biting into an apple, tugging on shoppers' coats, and they would shove her, telling her to go away. She would then return to her mother, who loudly scolded the girl in Romany for being a nuisance. This was to please her customers, women who sometimes stopped to peruse the blouses exhibited by the Roma sellers—these were not at all Romani style, adorned with lace and rhinestones, with ruffled sleeves, the kind of blouses in which people used to dance around bonfires in forest clearings. The ones sold by the Roma sellers were plain, white and yellow, with padded shoulders. Part of an outfit suitable for a secretary, an office clerk, or a businesswoman who could well sport such a blouse under an expensive suit and pretend it was purchased from the same store as the suit.

Martin had to buy some bell peppers, so he stood in a queue at the stall. There were two women before him. That was when the little Roma girl spotted him.

The girl kept staring at this tall figure carrying many grocery bags. After a while, she ran towards him and stood in a queue behind him, her head held high, eyes fixed on his back. She followed him until he paid for his shopping and shoved the veggies into a basket. Martin had noticed her right away and every now and then he turned to wink at her. She kept dead serious.

"What a girl you happen to have!"

The trader counted the money for the bell peppers.

When Martin turned towards the exit, the girl ran after him. Her mother, holding a bundle of blouses, did not notice.

"What do you want?" the young man turned around, kneeled, and placed his heavy bags on the ground.

He grabbed her hand. She grabbed his hand. She did not try to free herself. He looked into the wide-open black eyes of a young woman. He had never seen anything like it before.

DOG FOOD

Life is not all sad. Life, you know, is both happy and sad. There is no use looking at everything one-sidedly—such a perspective is just not true. Take dog food. I am reminded of the gentleman from the bus as I open a can of dog food. Chunks of beef in gravy, the jelly looking tasty, all the more so since I haven't had lunch yet today. A kind of stew. In Soviet times, stew was one of our most popular dishes—heart stew with grits or chicken lung or gizzard stew. Now it is very rare and only served in the cheapest of eateries. Tongue in horseradish sauce is also rare today, not to mention pig tails with mustard. I used to love nibbling at them, picking out meat from among unshaven tufts of pig's hair. Yummy!

Remarkably, my dog does not really like canned food. He prefers sausage scraps or leftover bones from dinner. I don't get it. I dip a fork into the can and fish out two pieces of meat from the jelly. They go into my mouth. Not salty enough, not salty at all; I chew again and taste the bone meal, which is a novelty for me, quite a doggy experience. I pour the rest into the dog's bowl, add some bread, stir it up. If he refuses to eat, tough luck—he will go hungry, and he cannot complain.

A phone call from my pal: "Look, there's this job coming, I am putting together a supplement for the anniversary of the Auschwitz camp liberation. Do you want to write something? I need to see your ideas within the next two days. If what you've got is good, I will publish it." I should do it, I am thinking. I know how to write about Auschwitz. Somehow, I know what it is about, though I have no idea why. I am not well-versed in the relevant literature—when it comes to Borowski, yes, we read him in high school, and it was hard. Then there was the matter of his suicide—was it because of Auschwitz, or perhaps due to the painful realisation that he had been used and fucked over by the Stalinists? And he was one of their lot, by the way.

Nałkowska. Yet another obligation. I was reminded of "Professor Spanner," the manufacturer of soap made out of people. A scene from one classroom period: Our teacher, Ms. Malinowska, was introducing something and said that an eminent professor, a very eminent professor, the most eminent of the eminent, had written something. That he had initiated it and that others followed and that was what we were looking at, blah, blah, blah . . . Then there was a whisper coming from the desk at the very back of the room:

"Professor Spanner..." and we all laughed.

And there was no more focus on the lesson, no more attention. Commotion. That was when I started drawing my friend Olgierd in the striped suit worn by Auschwitz prisoners in my notebook. I showed it to him. He scoffed. Unsavoury, all this. I have kept the drawing to this day.

"If you like, you can interview Zofia Posmysz," my article-procuring pal called me the next day. "It can be long, as long as nineteen thousand words."

That day when my friend called, as usual, I got on my bicycle and rode to work. I had had no idea those in my company were that ruthless. I have a Dutch bike with a rear pannier; I bought it myself in Amsterdam. The bicycle frame is beautiful, the paint gleaming black. When will this city finally have real bicycle lanes? I had wanted to develop my magazine, to publish new thematic supplements in large print runs, focusing on history and spectacular events, and they kicked me out.

"Bartek, Bartek, come in for a moment," came a voice from the publisher's office.

The editor-in-chief and my successor is a nice guy, but he has no balls. I wish him all the best. I started thinking about what's next in my professional life. I'm still looking. Marta has a good job as a cardiologist with a second-degree specialization. She earns a lot of money. That is good. I saved quite a bit myself during my years as the chief editor. Poverty and hunger do not loom over us. The children are growing, and there are new needs, but we also have a house in Zalesie which we rent out—our situation is far from gloomy.

I was doing various jobs, based on my extensive contacts within the industry—a TV show, a debate on the radio, a thematic insert printed in colour in a magazine; it had been all right. Still, I did not really know what to do next. Marta comforted me. Sometimes we would eat out and make plans for the future together over a shared meal. And as I tasted the Thai-style lamb, for a moment the taste of canned dog food was back with me. I did not mention this experience to my wife, as she would no doubt suspect I was developing depression, which would have scared her. She reads a lot of books on psychology, including ones that focus on successful family life.

I prepare for the interview. First, I call the writer. Her voice in the receiver is high but quiet. She consents to an interview.

"How does she feel?" I wonder. "Will I be able to write sixteen thousand? Or less?"

In books written by Posmysz, there are no insults directed at executioners, no complaints about her own fate. Instead, she attempts to explore the mentality of an SS man, a person who loves his dog and kills little children. When I was a child, my grandmother used to tell me that the Germans took small children by the legs and smashed their heads against the wall. Years later, I believed this was the old lady's imagination, influenced by communist propaganda. But today I walk into the biggest bookshop in the city and buy all the books they have on concentration camps. I leave the bookstore and head to a nearby park, where I sit on a bench. I turn the pages, look at the photographs. In Anja Lundholm's book, *Das Höllentor*, about Ravensbrück, I come across the following scene: an SS man stops a little boy, just a few years old, and talks to him, even plays with him. The child is no longer afraid of the man in uniform, when suddenly the tormentor grabs the boy's legs and smashes his head against the barracks' wall. Grandmother, you were right!

I do not mention any of this Auschwitz-related stuff to Marta. She has no wish to hear about genocide, though she does have a taste for violence—she devours crime stories one after another: Scandinavian, English, French, Polish, old-school and contemporary. There is a real proliferation of such literature today.

"Why is it that you can read about some psychopath cutting up a corpse, feasting on a piece, and burying the rest, but you don't want to learn what experiments Mengele performed?"

She gets all wound up: "You don't understand. Crime fiction is just entertainment, there is nothing real in it. And the crime itself is not so important, it is the circumstances—you learn a lot of details about the world, about people."

"What a silly thing to say," I retort. "Why should murder be entertainment? Who said it should be? Agatha Christie? Who could be so thick?"

We could reach no agreement then. And I dropped the topic because, why push it? I did not need Marta to be interested in death camps. Why should she be? She knew what she was made to learn in school. We have two children. You cannot force anyone to delve into the abnormality of those times. Knowing is one thing, delving in is quite another. That is what I am doing, because I was commissioned to do it. I make a fake cover for Anja Lundholm's book from wrapping paper and read it in bed before I go to sleep.

"On the 25th of January 1945, as Soviets liberated the Auschwitz camp, you were no longer there . . ."

"On the 18th of January we were led out of the camp and forced to walk towards the Third Reich. It was absurd. I kept wondering: What was the purpose for the Germans? There were Soviet planes flying around, and we walked and walked. We walked for three days—by then, there was no rail transport anymore. When we reached Włodzisław in Silesia, they crammed us into freight wagons, wide open—it was January, minus eighteen degrees Celsius. The train started the journey, and it was said that they tried to find a place for us in the camps along the way. I do not know how many people were on that train. Three days later we arrived at Ravensbrück. There was no room there either, so we were herded into something like a circus tent. There were no beds or toilets, not to mention *waschraums* or anything like that. Sheaves of straw were thrown on the brick floor, with no blankets, and we slept on them. We, Polish women, had to go find a toilet or a bathroom in other blocks, though the block leaders were not keen to let us."

"Prisoner Anja Lundholm, a German woman, author of the book *Das Höllentor*, recalls that the tent was where women and children were housed in 1944, following the Warsaw Uprising. Both women and children were dying. Lundholm and her fellow prisoners went as far as breaking into the SS women's sleeping quarters to get blankets and food. Have you met these women?"

"There were several thousand women in that tent—so they must have been there."

"What happened then?"

"Three weeks later, some of us were transported to the subcamp Neustadt-Glewe. It was comfortable there, and we were put in the former air staff quarters, next to the airport. There were no people there anymore, no aircraft either, but the barracks were decent, made of wood, with a toilet and a washroom. We no longer had to work, but the hunger was terrible. On the second of May, in the morning, we realized there were no more SS troops in the camp, and in the afternoon, the American soldiers came—it must have been a reconnaissance unit. They crossed the Elba River to assess the situation. In the evening, they brought us parcels. They warned us that the Russians were coming, that we should move across the river, which was the demarcation line. 'We are retreating from here,' they said. Two or three girls went with them. They were Polish women who had French citizenship. Then the Russians came, which was later called liberation, but we had, in fact, already been liberated."

We greet each other. Zofia Posmysz does not let me kiss her hand as she does not like the gesture. She is 92 with a pale complexion and narrow hands, meticulously styled grey hair. It is summer, and the writer is wearing a short-sleeved blouse, the tattoo visible. The digits on her skin are blurred, though perhaps it is just me as I try not to look that way. Still, they attract my gaze, pull me in, I don't know why.

"Did you drive here?" she asks.

"No."

"Then why don't we have a drink?"

I accept, and she fishes out a bottle of brandy from a cabinet, then brings some tonic from the kitchen.

"Do you prefer it undiluted? I, myself, like it with something."

I opt for brandy with something as well. While I pour the brandy, she adds the tonic. We drink. Where do we start? I have everything ready, jotted down in my notebook, but somehow I do not feel like opening it. I just turn on the recorder. Zofia is telling her story, gladly, even though she must have told it more than once or twice. As I listen, I am transported there, among the barracks, by the river, in which they waded knee-deep, to reach the camp hospital.

It is strange that the SS dog that Posmysz wrote about, the one that prisoners hung on a wire, which provoked fury and sobs from the SS women—"The bastards, criminals! We shall find out who they are! They will all end up in the gas chamber!"—that dog had more food than the people in the camp. He got porridge with meat, while they had bread with margarine and watery cabbage soup. I think: if only the prisoners had the kind of canned rations my dog gets now. And, by the way, my dog is not too keen to eat that food. Would not have it, any of it. Each can contains 1,250 grams of meat in jelly, and the people back then? They struggled to get an onion or a raw potato.

. . .

That, and things like that, are what I think about. I also ponder what my job should be, what my life could be, when one day someone calls me from an unfamiliar number.

"Hello, is this Marek Siwiński? My name is Beata Badurek."

There is a moment of silence and then the slightly trembling voice continues.

"I am calling you about something a bit unusual, but for me it is important. Your wife and my husband are dating. They are having an affair."

Here the small voice falls silent again, and I am shocked. We are both quiet for a while.

"Are you sure?"

"It has been going on for a long time. I found out a month ago, but even earlier I suspected something."

"How long?"

"I don't know exactly, but I suppose . . . a few months for sure, maybe longer."

More silence.

"I am calling you to ask that you talk to your wife. We have three children. I don't want my husband to . . . I don't want the children to lose . . ." she starts crying and hangs up.

From our balcony we can see the allotment gardens. In the summer, I sometimes gaze at this landscape for long moments at a time. I am gazing now and see nothing. Just emptiness, even after I take a deep breath. It is a warm evening. I stand there, breathing—there is nothing. I do not know for how long and then the dog suddenly yelps in the kitchen. Hungry. And I feel hungry as well. My wife is out, doing her evening shift, and she will come home late in the evening. After all, I can't expect someone who works so hard to make me dinners, while I am looking for something to do with my life. I can't expect the woman whom Badurek is fucking right now to take care of this whole household. Wait, wait, the name sounds familiar, do I know it? Badurek rings a bell, something in common, a long,

long time ago, a colleague at some internship. Wait, it is not that. No, I can't remember.

I pour the canned dog food into a bowl. It is chicken. I mix it with bread and put it on the floor, next to the fridge. The dog waggles his tail and sniffs at it, distrustful. He has become so picky, that son of a bitch. I think about Badurek and pour the chicken stew from the dog can on my plate—that's the kind of meal I'll have today. Should I heat it up in the microwave? No, it is better served cold. Quite like Warsaw-style pork loin, just need to add a bit of salt. A bit more. Now, it is good. I eat it with plain bread. What else do I need? I know what. I take a bottle of vodka from the cupboard and pour some into a regular glass because I don't feel like searching for a little vodka glass. I drink and eat dog food. And then, after the "stirrup drink," I take another swallow, this one for the "second leg," though I've gone nowhere on this journey. It is supposed to be premium vodka, it says "Russkij Standard" on the bottle. Maybe it is premium quality, I have no idea as I don't drink vodka at all, and neither does my wife, though we have plenty of vodka bottles. All are gifts Marta got from her grateful patients. We distribute them among friends, family, and are still always stocked on brandy, whisky, red and white wine, liqueurs—a cornucopia in the kitchen cupboard.

I poke my head into Kacper's room and nudge my shoulder against the doorframe. He is sitting with his computer. Klaudia is lying on her bed, reading. She is a big girl, turning fifteen this year. I go back to the kitchen. I feel the blood slowly surge to my head, and with it the first anger. Kacper is the boy who, at the age of three, spilled a cup of hot tea onto his head. It was our fault he pulled it off the table and now he has a red mark on his forehead. I feel drunk as if the cavalry is getting ready to charge into the valley. I go back to the kitchen, pour myself some more vodka—by my standards this is total drunkenness. But when she comes home from work—no, wait, when she comes back from fucking Badurek, I shall already be sleeping the sleep of the righteous, like Noah. And the damn Badurek will not provide me with cover, for which he shall be eternally damned.

The pennants are fluttering, the officers are about to utter their orders, the artillery positions must be taken. "'Forward, the Light Brigade! Charge for the guns!' an officer said. 'Into the valley of Death, rode the six hundred.'"

"Children, it is bedtime," I shout with a voice that does not sound like mine; I am stuck at the kitchen table.

In fact, I don't want to think about anything. I just wait for them to get to these guns. I see them riding into that Northern Valley.

> Cannon to right of them,
> Cannon to left of them,
> Cannon in front of them
>   Volleyed and thundered;
> Stormed at with shot and shell,
> Boldly they rode and well,
> Into the jaws of Death,
> Into the mouth of hell
>   Rode the six hundred.

They still have several hundred metres to cover. Will they make it? I put my head into my hands. I feel my stomach tighten. It must be the dog food.

Flashed all their sabres bare,
Flashed as they turned in air
Sabring the gunners there,
Charging an army, while
  All the world wondered.
Plunged in the battery-smoke
Right through the line they broke;
Cossack and Russian
Reeled from the sabre stroke
  Shattered and sundered.
Then they rode back, but not
  Not the six hundred.

* * *

"So, you are free, there is no camp anymore, the oppressors are gone. What did you think about then?"

"How to get home. That was my only concern, because there was no transport. The prisoners knocked down the gate, which we were unable to open, and we ran into the airport, all happy that it was freedom at last. But then it dawned on one of us: We got no bread for breakfast! So, we went back to the camp to get bread. That was how it happened."

"How did you get home?"

"On foot. We walked for three weeks, as far as Poznań, where we caught a train. Then all went their separate ways—that is, in our group of twenty. We had stayed together, though two of us unfortunately remained behind to celebrate the victory with the Russians and got alcohol poisoning. One of them, she was a Czech, died and the other, a Pole, who had survived two years in the camp—she went blind."

"What else do you remember from that passage?"

"We were led by Mrs. Perzanowska, a medical doctor from Auschwitz. I got to know her well at the camp. In 1944, I worked as a *schreiberin*—a clerk at the camp kitchen—and had access to food. If circumstances allowed, I would sneak something out of the storeroom and deliver it to the children's block or the hospital, where Doctor Perzanowska worked. She was quite thrifty and clever, people said she had been born in Odesa. In any case, she was fluent in Russian, which was very useful as we were making our way back to Poland. She had both foresight and courage. Whenever we stopped in a village for the night, she would always look for the Soviet secret police quarters, go there and say: 'Look, we are a group of Polish political prisoners from Auschwitz, your soldiers are assaulting us, do something.' And as it happened, on two occasions, we had Soviet soldiers standing guard. I could hear them threatening the men who wanted to get us. We avoided rape. I finally reached Kraków on the 24th of May, 1945."

The next day, I hear water running in the bathroom. Marta is taking her morning shower. I do not remember when she came back. I must have blacked out, hence the splitting headache. I venture into the kitchen to hydrate. The kids are still asleep, but they will wake up soon, then eat breakfast and go off to school. Maybe I will just dress quietly and run away? Remove myself from their lives, since I am no good as a husband, as a man. Why should Kacper witness that, why should Klaudia . . . ?

I drink water from a plastic bottle. It is so, so good! Ramses is pacing around in the hallway. I quickly put on my coat and grab the dog leash. On the third floor the elevator stops and Marek gets in. We are neighbours and sometimes have a barbecue together. He works as an analyst at some company. All in all, a nice guy, but I am definitely not fit for any of that today. I try not to look him in the eye. We nod, but he seems to have sensed something.

"Are you feeling unwell?"

"I might be developing something, I have a headache and shivers."

"You should go to bed. It must be a virus, and you need to sleep it off . . . I had it last month."

Back at home, I go into the kitchen, put on the kettle.

"What's going on? Are you feeling unwell?"

My wife has a towel wrapped around her body and another around her head. She is standing there, looking at me, while I look at her. I see a woman in her thirties, slender and tanned, with long legs, droplets of water on her thighs. I see her anew, a woman whose body I know by heart, and yet as of today, she has become a stranger. It is as if an eerie shadow has passed through the kitchen and changed the wife forever. The wife? Is it my wife? No, it is no longer my wife, it is a completely new construct, a Japan-made premium-quality sex doll that few can afford. Including a certain Badurek.

I start talking to her, but I cannot hear my voice. Eventually, I break through into my own consciousness, but I still have no clue what I might be talking about. Finally, I hear:

"I think I have a fever, I need to lie down."

Marta approaches and puts her hand on my forehead. My lips are chapped and my tongue stiff from the booze I drank yesterday, but she won't notice—she has never seen me hungover like this. Unless she has seen Badurek, but how should I know? The indecency of the situation also stems from the fact that Marta is about to go to work and I am supposed to work at home, and I cannot even finish my interview with Zofia Posmysz about her experience in the Auschwitz concentration camp.

"Will you have something to eat? Should I make scrambled eggs?"

"I will take a fever medicine and this other thing . . . go and lie down. Do I have any appointments in town today?" I just say that to make myself talk. Not to look at her. So that she does not say anything.

But she does.

"I need to go to the clinic a little early today, then I have my shift at the hospital, remember? The lunch is ready, you just need to cook some rice."

Klaudia hangs around the kitchen, eating her cereal. I add some dry dog food pellets to the dog's bowl and wonder if Marta is equally caring towards the other guy. During her training days and trips abroad, does she make sure her lover is well fed and nicely dressed? I hear Ramses munching his food under the table, and something is rising in me and if I do not stop it, it will explode. I need time, much more time. I need to stay vigilant, damn vigilant, and not let the circumstances get the best of me like they have this morning.

Off she goes. She kisses me goodbye, perhaps sensing the Russkij Standard? I wash down headache pills with coffee and take a shower. I stay there for a long time. I am about to wank, just like Kevin Spacey in *American Beauty*, but then I get so sad that the thought of it evaporates. I towel myself dry and think of Zofia Posmysz. There were love affairs and cheating in Auschwitz, too. In her book she wrote about a girl who had a tin medallion from her beloved, even though jewellery was strictly forbidden. My aunt told me once that they were shot at, she fell, and then crawled out from under a pile of corpses. I suppose it might have been during the evacuation of the camp, the death march. She went through hell as well. After the war she started drinking more and more. I remember the tattoo on her forearm. Zofia's tattoo has blurred over time, but she makes no effort to hide it. In the summer, she wears short-sleeved blouses.

Freedom has a scent like the top of a newborn baby's head . . . The songs are in your eyes, I see them when you smile . . .

Bono is king. Marta and I attended his concert at Bemowo. The kids stayed with my mother. Good old times. We used to listen to music together . . . now we do nothing, absolutely nothing. How come? When did it become like this? I had not noticed. I was busy, working hard, developing the magazine, publishing hot news supplements. I sold half a million copies each week and then got fired. I started wondering how to reinvent myself, while my wife had yet another orgasm lying in Badurek's arms.

Right. Making the bed. I shall not go back to bed. The headache has subsided a bit. I turn on the computer because I need to finish that interview, then a call to Zofia Posmysz to authorise the content. Great clouds float by just outside the window. One grey at the bottom, dirty yellow at the top. Who knows where it is heading. Maybe towards me, maybe towards my wife, my children. I turn off the music. I need silence. I hear the quiet voice of Zofia Posmysz from the recorder. I cannot picture her at all, except in that striped camp suit. For years she had a job running the literary broadcast on the news; she'd led a normal life, had a husband, wrote books, was part of the Polish Writers' Union, received awards and medals. She took holidays. In 1945, Posmysz made her debut, publishing her memoirs, *Znam katów z Belsen* (*I have known the butchers of Belsen*), but she is most famous for her 1962 book *Pasażerka* (*The Passenger*).

Ramses has joined me. He wags his tail and jumps onto the sofa. He curls up, a black ball, glancing at me. A fly goes by. The dog pricks up his ears, then sighs and closes his eyes.

"How did you end up in Auschwitz?"

"I did nothing serious, not like having a gun or even a radio. The occupier closed not only universities and colleges but also secondary schools, and young people of school-age had to work. I registered with the Arbeitsamt and started working as a waitress in a casino. I was 19. At that time, there were already secret classes, or secret education. I managed to get in touch with these people. The classes took place in various places, mostly private flats, with different teachers, some from outside the General Government area. The boys in my teaching group must have been in touch with the underground, and they sometimes gave us news from the fronts."

"They caught you during random searches?"

"Luckily we came early, otherwise all twenty of us would have been arrested. They caught four people, three boys and me."

"And what were you doing in Auschwitz, to which block were you assigned?"

"Block number eight. In the beginning, Polish women were only allowed to work in the outer commandos, outside the camp. It was hard work in the fields. The soil in Auschwitz is, as farmers say, heavy, rich. By spring, the furrows that were ploughed in the autumn would become hard as stone. No one had tended the fields. We broke them up with hoes. On the first day several girls fainted. We carried the ones that did not regain consciousness back to the camp. Then we were transferred and made to cut rushes on the Soła River. The Germans said it had to be cleared. This was better for us, as you could rest for a while among the riverside reeds. The weather was beautiful, it was June, and there were not enough *Aufseherinnen* to supervise us all. One day, as we were returned to the camp, we discovered that one girl was missing. It was clear that she had crossed the river and that the dogs had lost track on the shore. We were terrified, we knew that absconding was punishable by decimation of fellow prisoners."

"And what happened next?"

"That time we were spared. Our commando of 200 people was assigned to the penal company in Budy, a village four kilometres away from the main camp. We were housed in the former school buildings, not adapted for such purposes, so we slept on mattresses directly on the floor and in the attic. It was safer in the attic because the German women prisoners at Auschwitz would rush into the building after the gong for roll call and lash out, especially at those who were downstairs. They were psychopaths, they bullied us."

"Anyone else?"

"One of the officers, we called him Till Eulenspiegel because he had protruding ears. He was a sadist and would beat people for no reason, pound them with his fists, and when his victim was lying on the ground, he would keep kicking until they stopped moving. Once he was done lashing out, he would call in the German women prisoners to finish off the job. After two months in the penal company, only 143 out of 200 people returned to the Birkenau camp."

"What was most memorable?"

"The man on the wire. At 6 a.m. the wires were still live and we were rushed to the field. The scream a person makes as they are electrocuted is horrid, a kind of moan. Indescribable."

I felt hungry. For the first time that day. The dog followed me to the kitchen, a worried look in his eyes. I cut off a piece of salceson we bought for the dog and threw it into the bowl. After a while, I cut another piece for myself. If I file for divorce, she will get custody over the children. In a Polish court of law, I will lose the case and will have to move out. The children will be shocked, though they already understand a lot. I put the piece of salceson on a slice of bread and douse it in ketchup. After the first bite I sense that they add bone meal here too, there is not enough salt. Ramses has already devoured his piece and is looking at me again. I won't share my piece—it is mine, and mine alone! Just for me! Marta used to be mine alone, but not anymore.

The weather has been weird today.

As I walk down the street in our neighbourhood, I feel I've reached a dead end, and at the same time, I realize how free I am. There are so many options on the horizon that I feel trepidation. At Puławska street I turn left, the tram rings, a large crow sits down on a bush and opens its beak. I could now walk up to the hospital, ask Badurek to follow me outside, and punch him in the face. I could, but I know I won't. I could start a fight with my wife, complete with insults and slapping her face in front of the children. Our neighbours would hear the screams. I know I won't do it. I could call Badurek's wife, tell her she is a stupid cunt, and threaten that if I hear from her again, I'll have a serious conversation with her husband, and does she want their children to see their daddy's face bruised? I could, but I know I won't. I could go directly to a brothel, take two whores and in that threesome ponder vindictively the deeds of my unfaithful spouse. I could, but I know I won't. I could call my in-laws, who live in Radom, and tell them everything, which would cause a family-wide commotion. I could tell my mother, who would also start a ruckus. I could, but I know that I won't. That is my freedom. I could sit here and just open my beak like that crow. Like the crow, I could keep turning my head and look stupidly at the whole fucked-up world. And that's what I decide to do.

"Do you have a lot of homework?" I ask Kacper when he comes home.

"Just maths. And history," he corrects himself.

"What homework in history? Show me your notebook!"

I read the instructions: "In bullet points, write about how the Germans persecuted Poles and Jews." So, we have come to a point when weeks and months of suffering, the unspeakable and unthinkable anguish of the days in the camps, the nightmare of the nights spent on camp bunk beds, the bodies tortured by lice, the bestiality of guards, all this is now to be put into bullet points. Children separated from their mothers—one bullet point. Drowning someone in a barrel of faecal matter—another bullet point. Beaten to death by an inmate supervisor—bullet point. Gas chamber—bullet point. Removal of ovaries from women—yet another bullet point. Spotted typhus—bullet point. Starvation leading to insanity—last bullet point. Homework done. But what do these bullet points have to do with what actually happened? Nothing at all.

I ask Kacper to do his homework while I sit at my desk and look around. As I had prepared for my interview with Posmysz, I gathered lots of camp-related literature, and now I reach for a book in a striped suit cover that I had purchased long ago from a drunkard in the West Railway Station. I start reading *Oczami dziecka* (*Through the eyes of a child*) by Stella Müller-Madej. Bubik, her friend from the Kraków ghetto, displaced from Dresden and owner of a German

Shepherd dog, used to call her Stellusha. When Stella fell ill, he persuaded a police officer to accompany him as he left the ghetto to buy lemons for lemonade he wished to serve her. Such a nice pal, Bubik, a real friend. KL Płaszów, and the image of couples kissing by the barracks. Amon Göth, the demon of the place, a character combining features of a gloomy Egyptian crypt dweller with a stinking coward, gunning defenceless women down as they return to the camp after a whole day of gruelling toil. And the children that had been smuggled into the camp hidden in backpacks, small ones. They sit quietly on the bunk beds, terrified. "Hide Samuel. Or they will come and shoot Samuel, bang-bang," the child goes on and on, trying to hide under the bunks.

Slamming the door, Kacper goes out to walk Ramses. Klaudia should be back soon. It is time to put the rice on the stove, reheat the dinner prepared by the unfaithful mum. I decide to boycott the chicken stew with wood ear mushrooms that she prepared. I tear the lid off another can of dog food and, not even sitting down, I stand near the fridge and swallow the jellied meat. I gulp it down in a hurry. I decide to open a bottle of red. I pour myself a full glass and taste the fine drink. Then I sprinkle some salt onto a plate and dip the jellied portions of meat into it. It tastes much better now. Now I am in KL Płaszów, in a barracks where the children only eat inedible cabbage soup and a piece of black bread dabbed with margarine spread. The appalling cruelty of the tormentors, the mass murder machine deployed to ensure domination of some over others, torturing people into submission, into renouncing life, their most wonderful gift from God.

After stuffing my stomach, I pour the rest of the jellied meat into Ramses's bowl then take another sip of wine. The meal was cold, but I feel a nice warmth radiating from my stomach.

"And?"

Klaudia is a pretty girl. She looks like her mother with long, shiny ash-blond hair. She is about to turn fifteen this year. Conceived before we got married, at a campsite in Saumur when Marta and I were visiting the châteaux of the Loire, or that is what we assume happened. It was a warm evening, we had just eaten grilled vegetables and were drinking boxed wine, the cheapest there was. The sun was setting behind the tall trees, and I looked in Marta's eyes and noticed a hint of navy blue.

"And what?" replied my daughter.

"Generally, is everything okay?"

"I'm fine, it is just that on Friday I'd like to stay overnight at Magda's. You know, movie night . . ."

I was already asleep when Marta came to bed and I felt her body next to mine. Without thinking, I reached out and put my arm around her. Her hand on my back, her breath on my cheek. The first kiss was long, a bit like a spasm. I pulled her towards me, Marta climbed on top of me, and I began to caress her breasts. There's a clearing in the deep, deep forest that is hard to find, yet everyone wishes to get there as it is sunny, and you can bask in the warm rays for a long time. Nearby, there is a lake with floating islands. Marta was next to me again, and I immediately lay down on top of her.

In the morning I had a tormenting dream. My whole family was at a party—Kacper, Klaudia—we were waiting for someone. Marta was also waiting for him. He was supposed to be late, her new husband, still recovering from his injury, and we were all worried about what had happened to his little hand. Finally, he came, his arm in a sling, and he and Marta kissed, and I realized that they were together, that she was no longer with me. I woke up, got up, went to the bathroom.

"What made you survive? Was it hope that you would be free? Faith?"

"Before the war, when we spent holidays at my grandparents, my mum used to take me to Kalwaria Zebrzydowska to the Marian paths. My grandfather would ready the cart pulled by his white horse and on the 15th of August we would ride to the fair. My childhood was like this, full of extraordinary experiences. In the chapel dedicated to the Third Fall of Christ, there is an altar with a life-size statue of Christ lying under the cross. I remember a particular afternoon. The chapel was full of people praying silently—great silence. I must have been four at the time. I was looking at Jesus and at one point I saw him raise his head. I started calling out to my mother that Jesus was getting up. There was a commotion. My mum started to shush me. I was very moved. But when I was in the camp, inside the wire fence, I recalled something else. We had a very strict priest who taught us religion. We feared him a little bit. One day, he suggested that for the next nine months, on the first Friday of each month, we should all go to church for confession and to receive Holy Communion. There was silence in the classroom and I fired a question: 'And why should we, Father?' 'Because, my child,' he replied, 'anyone who does is guaranteed not to die without receiving the sacraments.'"

"This assurance guided me in Auschwitz. After all, I had performed this novena, and I knew that I would not die there, because there were no sacraments in the camp. With this in mind, I made it through spotted fever and dysentery."

"How long did you stay ill?"

"I ran a high fever for ten days. When I came round, the fever began to drop. The order of things imposed by the Germans meant there was no medicine, not enough water, but there were thermometers, and nurses were assigned from among the prisoners. These assigned prisoners were supposed to provide us with bedpans even on the top bunks. Among these so-called nurses, there was Maria, a Polish woman. She came with the second transport from Warsaw. She was much older than me. She would climb into the top bunk bed to feed me soup to keep me hydrated. Maybe that was why I recovered from the typhoid? One day she didn't come, and when she wasn't there the following days either, I asked another assigned nurse what had happened to her. I learned that she had been taken to the Politische Abteilung, which meant to the Gestapo in the main camp, which meant death. She never came back. I never learned her surname or what her trade was."

"Typhoid in the camp spelled an epidemic . . ."

"Indeed. And when the SS officers started falling sick, the camp authorities decided to do something about it. They created a commando of imprisoned doctors. I was there, ill with dysentery. One of the doctors, a Pole, Doctor Mąkowski (as I found out later), realized that it was the beginning of the end. He told me to survive one more night and that he would bring me some medicine the next day. I lay awake, believing that he would come. He did come and brought something—some drops that he must have illegally procured from the SS hospital. The diarrhoea stopped. After the war I tried to find him but failed. In the 1960s, I happened to meet a woman I knew from the hospital barracks. I asked if she knew the whereabouts of Doctor Mąkowski. It turned out that he was working in Szczecin, in a hospital, and since she also lived in Szczecin, I asked her to tell him I was grateful and that I had been looking for him, that I was writing a story about him. She did, but the doctor replied that he could not recall me, which was no surprise—I was not the only person he had assisted in the camp."

"What prompted you to write about all this?"

"I did not intend to, it came about by coincidence. I worked at the radio, in the literary department. I was a reporter. One day, I was told to write a text about flying to Paris. It was when they first launched the Warsaw-Paris flight connection. In Paris, the head pilot told me to go explore the city before we returned to Poland. So I did. And on the Place de la Concorde, among the throng of tourists calling to each other, I heard: 'Erica, komm, wir Fahrem schon!' It was a high-pitched voice, harsh and unpleasant. That was the voice of the SS woman guard that supervised us in the camp. I froze. It was 1959, and I had been following all the Nazi criminals' trials that started in 1945, but I had never seen or heard about her. What was I to do? Should I look for a police officer and point her out? Or maybe greet her? I turned away. No, it was not her. But following my return, I couldn't stop thinking about her and then my husband told me: just write about it. I wrote a radio broadcast, *The Passenger*, and that was how it started."

"What did you think of your persecutors back in the camp?"

"You had to be afraid of them, you had to avoid meeting them. Meeting one of them could spell death. But most of the SS guards were women who simply applied for the job and got it, perhaps because it was well-paid? Maybe they did not really know what the job actually involved? The head SS woman guard behaved like this: she followed the regulations to the letter. As long as you did not break the rules, everything was fine. Sometimes I think I wished to see good in these people, something human, and some met this expectation. In my first weeks in the camp, when one day I got punched in the head by an SS man and the girls had to carry me back from the field into the camp, I remember that at the gate I heard the words '*Mein Gott, so jung!*' and I saw an SS cap right above me. I thought, if an SS woman can feel pity, then not everyone is evil."

"What was it, Auschwitz?"

"They say that in previous historical periods there were other hecatombs. But in our times, they invented gas with which to kill people. In Norman Mailer's book *The Castle in the Forest*, the story about Adolf Hitler is narrated by Satan, who writes about his youth and the education through which he had shaped this individual. It was all based on the criminal idea of race."

"Do you still have dreams about the camp?"

"Not anymore. Since I started writing, I stopped dreaming about the camp. It was a kind of liberation, self-therapy. As I come towards the end of my life, I have gone back to Auschwitz. I collaborated with the International Youth Meeting Centre there, so in fact I am still stuck in that time. And do you know what was my most frequent dream before that? That I lost my job at the camp storeroom! And it was because I worked in the camp kitchen that I hoped I may survive."

In the morning, I notice that Marta has scratches on her back. If I ask her about it, she would have to lie that it was me. But it wasn't me. I have never scratched her back, and would never do it so forcefully. It is definitely Badurek's signature.

Klaudia in a striped suit, Kacper imprisoned in the camp, I thought to myself while brewing my first coffee. Why assume it will never happen again, and not be even worse. It took place seventy years ago—is that that long ago in history? It is ridiculously recent. Once upon a time people believed the Pharaoh's rule was eternal or that Rome would rule the world until the very end. And look what happened. None of it remains, I mean besides ruins, which I used to visit with Marta and then with the kids—we once spent our holidays in Egypt. Klaudia wanted to climb the Great Pyramid of Giza, we all rode camels, we waited in line to get as close as possible to the Sphinx. Did it say anything that might have saved our relationship? The Sphinx could not care less, after all, he is keeping an eye on the tombs of the country's rulers, long plundered by robbers, and on top of that his nose is missing. Klaudia looked around for scorpions and Kacper wanted to buy souvenirs peddled in great abundance by the locals. Fuck, why am I reminded of all this now, in the kitchen, after I have spent a night with my wife in a warm bed? Perhaps other memories would be more appropriate at this point? Those of Wanda Kalinowska-Giorgi's, for example, about her father, who told her that he had been in Mauthausen-Ebensee, that they assigned him to corpse removal in the crematorium; it was then he had stopped being human, he was just ever so hungry. Where was God then? Where is God? In Auschwitz, during a roll call, they hanged two Jews and a Pole. The Jews died quickly, but it took the Pole several minutes to die in prolonged agony. Where is He? This Christ of yours? He is here, hanging on the gallows, said one of the prisoners.

The smell of coffee permeates the kitchen. Marta has put on a blouse, to hide any scratch marks I might ask about. She smiles at me and I smile at her. We kiss for a long time, after all, last night we were so tender towards each other. Klaudia and Kacper are about to leave for school and she starts work in the afternoon. She must have incredible sexual needs, that is my view, or maybe I flatter myself? I wrap my arm around Marta's waist, she lifts her leg and entwines it behind me. We need to wait for the children to leave the house.

Marta packs Kacper's breakfast in a box and puts it in his backpack. It is uncanny, I feel no revulsion towards her, and she—even though she has sex with Badurek—she still craves making love to me. The children are off to school, and we lie in the bedroom again. It is all over now. The incomparable sadness. That is why I let my thoughts on our situation linger, I know I can't help it. I lie down, feeling the hard mattress under me, a nice sensation, and this lightness, it lifts me up, allows me to relax. Marta is getting dressed. She does it in a lazy fashion, takes her time choosing underwear, I have the feeling she does it on purpose. She puts on her stockings, which is strange on a weekday like today.

"Who do you dress like that for?"

"No one, why should you ask?"

"I am just talking. Why? Do you think I don't know the way guys look at you in the hospital? Patients, doctors . . ."

"Me? Do you know how many young nurses there are? The trainee women doctors?" my wife laughs.

Then in the bathroom, she takes a long time to do her makeup. She kisses me goodbye. And leaves. I am a bit hungry. In the very bottom drawer of the fridge there is some dog food. I slide the box out and read the label: Active Pet. Chicken meat and liver pâté. I peel off the aluminum foil. The pâté is blood-coloured. I scoop some with a fork and taste it. Very high bone meal content, but it works for me. I spread the dog pâté on the bread, add two onion rings. Salt. It tastes great! Nothing else tastes like this, and if those people wearing striped suits had such grub, how many would not have starved to death—I think of them again. About that hunger, that was torture. I sip my breakfast coffee with milk and sugar. The day begins.

I should take a walk, get some air before everyone gets back home. Ramses is bouncing in the hallway.

"Come on, boy!"

I put him on a leash and we go out. I may go to the park, to walk under the trees by the Warszawianka sports centre. The weather is good. We walk briskly, then I remove the leash and the dog runs across the lawn. Tall chestnut trees and no place to sit, as all the benches have been taken by hobos. And in the furthest corners of the park there are no benches whatsoever.

I stand under a tree and dial a number.

"Hello?" the voice is trembling and seems to come from behind a veil.

"Good morning." I identify myself and give my reason for calling.

"And what time could you come?"

We agree to meet that afternoon. Zofia Posmysz says she has a lot of comments for me to incorporate into my text. We will discuss it. She invites me to visit her at home again. Ramses finds a piece of old brick and brings it to my feet. He has saliva all over his snout. I kick the brick and the dog immediately runs after it. He fetches it. I kick it away again. This goes on for a while. At home, I will have to wipe his face.

When I return home, I give the children lunch, brush my teeth, and leave. I take the tram to Bank Square, then past the Hipoteka and up the hill. This is the route I chose, although I could have opted for Długa Street. Homeless people are waiting for soup to be served by the church on Miodowa Street. They stand in small groups, having a smoke. They don't look at me or at each other, but past me or directly at the street, at the yellow bus, at the cars. The traffic light changes. A navy-blue cloud floats towards Krasiński Square. I cross the street.

"Are you driving?" I hear again when I sit in a chair at a small table.

Zofia is pouring brandy again, then she fills the glasses with tonic. A printout of the interview is in front of us, things crossed out all over, many added notes. We begin to discuss it. Zofia reads the text and the added comments and her voice is trembling. I mark my version, indicating where to insert her notes. Of course, she will also let me have her copy. A few hours' work and I should be done in one night, no problem. Tomorrow afternoon, the authorised interview is due to be submitted to the editor, but Zofia seems to trust me—she says I do not need to show her the revised text.

We are almost finished when the doorbell rings. Zofia is visibly energised.

"It is my colleague, the Austrian journalist Maria Bichler. You two can meet!"

The woman is in her thirties. She is wearing a red woolen dress and black tights. Her dark hair is tied back. We shake hands. What is her face like? Pale complexion, nice dark-framed eyes. I cannot say anything else about her features, I do not wish to seem to examine her. I take a sip from the glass. We sit at the table.

Maria is a translator and often accompanies Zofia on her travels in Europe when she attends reading sessions and author's meetings. She does not want brandy and tonic. She laughs out loud as she recounts their adventure in Klagenfurt. She crosses her legs. I feel a nice pressure in my loins and think for a moment that I could hit on this Austrian woman, maybe with success. As long as she is single, I could get my revenge on dear Marta. The thought passes as suddenly as it comes. Maria Bichler is still laughing—she is in good mood—and Zofia is also more cheerful now, with a kind of new sparkle in her dark eyes, these recent recollections have revived her memory, invaded the room, and are now with us. Maria and Zofia are planning another trip, to Vienna, and they talk about it for a while, then about the foundation where Zofia works. Then we chat about Polish literature translations into German.

It is time for me to go. I collect my papers and say goodbye to Maria Bichler. She looks me straight in the eye. Zofia walks me to the door. She holds my hand firmly when I want to kiss hers. She will have none of it. Back in the street, I feel a warm breeze on my cheek and walk towards Krakowskie Przedmieście. The streetlights are already on. Silhouettes in yellow and pink. Mine among them. I look at the buses passing me by, at the illuminated façades of the townhouses. The street leads somewhere, I walk ahead, sometimes looking at people who are just like me.

. . .

I have never told Marta that I knew of her infidelity. I also never heard from Badurek's wife again. I have no idea how long the hospital lovers were together, when they broke up, what happened next. I do not think our children sensed anything. Right after the events I described here, I landed a nice job in television, worked on a show about treasure hunters and travelled all over Poland. I was a guest in my own home. It was fine with me, at least for the first few months. Years passed. And then more years. I was promoted to programming director of a TV station. I felt good at work, and worked even more. Eventually, Klaudia moved out of the family home, and Kacper met a French woman and they settled in Bordeaux. A few years before my retirement, I bought a house in Kashubia and, after a while, I just moved there. Alone. I was retired by then. Marta stayed in our flat in Warsaw and, even though my children urged me in their emails to make her move in with me, I did not care. In their eyes, I was an insensitive bastard. Tough luck, apparently, it was meant to be. I had peace and quiet. The surface of the lake was mine alone day in, day out. The wind rustled in the reeds. This is how things came to an end.

THE VILLAGE BENEATH THE SAND

The street goes up. Heavy traffic, cars and motorbikes. On both sides of the street there are shops and restaurants. The smell of fried fish, exhaust fumes, hot pavement. She does not have the strength to walk uphill. Sweat beads on her forehead. She takes a seat at a café and does not care whether orders are placed at the bar or if someone waits on the tables.

Amber. It glistens on a ring, reflecting the harsh sunlight. She gazes at the stone—it has been with her for so long. It replaced her wedding ring after the divorce, thirty years ago now. There are some flecks in the amber—strange, fish-scale-like particles that have survived for hundreds of thousands of years. And they will continue to be there once she is gone.

"What can I get you?" the waitress has a pleasant voice.

She orders water with ice and lemon. There is lots of traffic in this alley. She doesn't like it. She regrets opting for this way to the beach, but it is a shortcut from her guesthouse. She first came here with Mikołaj, when he was little, a year before the divorce. He was four. Even then, her ex-husband preferred to spend his holidays in his own way, although she still believed he would return to her. She did her best, she even made love to him every single day, but did not manage to keep him. Such a pathetic, nearly faded memory. It was laughable. When she first came here, the streets were quieter. Not so many Warsaw-dwellers were flocking here back then. Old history. Now there is traffic and a throng of people walking, lots of prams with children.

Her favourite part of going to the beach is to stretch out on a towel and fall asleep, surrendering to the sun. No thinking, no planning for the next few days, no worrying about whether it will be sunny tomorrow. Sunscreen applied, one-piece swimsuit on, she hides behind a screen. Just the sky above, the calm sea, the fine waves. The hum of the sea. The possibility of a swim.

The walls of her room in a guesthouse run by the Verbites are white. These are the monk quarters where missionaries rest when they come back from their various placements around the world. Just recently one of them talked about his stay in Colombia during a sermon at Mass in the chapel. Drug cartels and leftist guerrilla troops in the mountains. Priests can get murdered there, but only if they meddle in politics. The ordinary locals—the young man wearing the priest's robe said—are wonderful, kind, grateful for the work done by devoted volunteers like him.

When she returns from the beach, she stares at the ceiling. Yesterday, there was a large black spider there. She whisked it away using her shirt. Silence. Her window looks onto the lagoon. There is a crucifix on the wall. Her son, Mikołaj, now also works in a foreign country. He is building roads in Jordan. He and his wife have lived there for three years now. He wanted her to visit them over the summer holidays, but she refused. Too far away, too hot, she said— she stayed in the country and came here. For the last ten years, she hadn't visited this village. She preferred to go somewhere else. But something has attracted her now, maybe because the Verbites offer accommodation at very affordable prices, the living conditions seem good. There is peace and quiet. It is all very cultured, no yelling next door, no disco music. And the beaches are beautiful, wide and clean, no glass from broken beer bottles or used condoms.

She favours the spot just outside the harbour, in the bend naturally formed by the dunes. She does not mind the cries of the seagulls circling above. She watches their erratic flight and subconsciously imagines a composition emerging in the sky. Since she closed and sold her studio, she has no wish to paint, but paintings still take over her imagination, appearing at different moments of the day, those enticing images: The roots sticking out from under the layer of sand in the surrounding woods—where she went for walks after lunch— treetops, and the misty shore behind the lagoon that she saw from the balcony as she inhaled the smoke from her first morning cigarette, though the priests do not allow smoking in their guesthouse.

Yesterday she met one of them. He lives in the room opposite to hers. There is a long clean corridor lined with grey terracotta tiles. On the walls are framed maps of African, Asian, and South American countries, portraits of missionaries, some of them blessed, some saints. This man from another room in her corridor, with a tired face and stubble which has grown for several days now, probably also thinks about sainthood—Father Dariusz, as he introduced himself in the canteen—usually wears civilian clothes, an unbuttoned polo shirt, sunglasses, but when she met him gliding quietly down their corridor one morning, he was wearing a cassock with a wide black belt. He was on his way to the chapel to celebrate Mass. At the corners of his mouth, as always, there was a shadow of a smile, so striking when paired with the tiredness of his grey eyes.

The undulations of the sandspit were extraordinary. Covered by mixed forest, they formed deep ravines, perfect for cycling, walking, and basking in the glades. One could then go down to the sea and cool off on the beach. She would spend her afternoons there, meeting other people, whole families, though she was always alone. Years ago, together with her little Mikołaj, she made a trip to a village eleven kilometres away, the last one before the border that crossed the narrow strip of land between the sea and the lagoon. They ate fish and bathed in the sea; the beach was wide and clean. They hitchhiked on their way back. When was that? Blank memory. At home, she kept a few black and white photographs from that time. Back then, she was earning quite well, selling a lot of paintings, mainly images of roses in vases, the alimony payments were regular.

The road to the village meanders. On either side there is a dense forest, illuminated by the rays of the young sun. It is strange that it is home to all sorts of animals: wild boar, deer, and a chimera from Arezzo—lion's eyes glinting ominously in the head of a goat with evil, fiendish eyes growing out of its left side. She wakes up suddenly, drenched in sweat. Lilac light streaming in from the lagoon through the window. She gets up, takes off her damp shirt, and changes quickly. She hears some sound from the corridor, a kind of stifled squeal, perhaps singing. She opens the door quietly, just a bit, and steps barefoot into the corridor. The sound is coming from Father Dariusz's room. She moves closer but cannot identify the sounds. They are very quiet, one following another.

She goes back to bed, falling asleep very quickly. The next day she observes the young Verbite priest as he sips his coffee, spreads butter on his bread roll, and tells her about his recent stay in the Congo and how he contracted malaria—she sees him with new eyes. She responds with a smile but does not say anything.

On the beach that day, she looks tenderly at others bathing and basking in the sun, as if they belong to a completely different world, totally alien, which would never ever merge with her reality again. The sand glistens softly and small clouds gather in the sky. She sits on a towel, smoking, gazing at the dark blue horizon. She stays like this all morning, but later, when she is in the forest, she looks at the pines, birches, and beeches with astonishment. She does not recognize them. The mood is solemn, like on the day of her first Holy Communion or her wedding. Overwhelmed, she knows that she cannot possibly return to the guesthouse just now.

She goes into a restaurant and studies the menu. The waiter approaches her and she orders fish soup, salad, and a small carafe of white wine. She had a heart attack over a year ago and her cardiologist recommended consuming small amounts of white wine. As she waits, she reads the short tourist guide entry featured at the end of the menu:

> Schmergrube—a village that is known to have once been located near ours, most likely around the highest hill on the spit, called the Camel's Hump, which offers a view of both the sea and the lagoon. The village of Schmergrube was inhabited by fisher folk, it had a brick church erected in the very centre. It is unclear what happened, whether it was a sudden natural disaster or perhaps a slow process of dunes shifting, but in the 17th century, the entire village, including the church, was buried beneath the sand. To date, no archaeological work has been carried out at the site.

She recalled that many years ago she wished to climb the Camel's Hump but failed to find the path. No one could tell her how to get there. It was different back then. Perhaps people were afraid to provide information. The site was part of a border buffer zone, after all. One could sometimes see the military patrols coming to the village, checking the holiday makers' papers. Now, it has all changed. It is good, she thinks, that my Mikołaj has found such a good job abroad, and that he can afford everything he needs. But there are still no grandchildren.

She sips her fish broth, musing that she is still here—life already passed, child-rearing passed, painting passed. Even the socialist regime is undone, just like her health, and she is still coming to the seaside, sunbathing, walking in the woods, drinking white wine at a table covered with a tasteful cream tablecloth, and thinking about the Camel's Hump.

Back in her room, she checks the walls for spiders, opens the balcony door, and looks out at the nighttime lagoon. Lights, white and green, glitter on the other shore. She closes the door behind her and lights a cigarette. She makes an ashtray out of a Pepsi can. Just beyond the main entrance to the guesthouse, on the left, is the chapel: a small room, white walls, a couple of rows of stacked chairs with red padding. She has popped in there several times. There is a little red lamp in front of the tabernacle. She has even considered praying, all these years later. Following her divorce, she had stopped practicing religion. That was another century, another era. It stayed that way. She would go to church only now and then, more often after the Holy Father passed away, but then the general mood made everyone go, only a heartless person would not feel the loss. But then she stopped going again. In her world, emotions were subdued, and everything had its place, its time, its meaning, and its lack of meaning. Religion gave no meaning to the days and months. Occasionally, there was a thought or a mood that may have originated from between the lines of a poem she had read, or shining from the margins of a novel she was reading, in a painting by an old master, Rembrandt especially, whose work she valued most highly.

The last time she looked into the chapel, there was a priest sitting there. In silence, he turned the pages of his breviary. And in him, in his figure, there was silence as well. She felt it very clearly. Intuition had never yet failed her—in painting, space and air are the same thing. Now, in her room, she thinks about a painting by Boznańska, with a nun, dressed in white, kneeling before a crucifix lying on the ground. The candles burning. She is quite sure it was actually the same scene she had seen in the chapel.

A cool breeze made her wrap her bathrobe tightly around her body. She put out the cigarette against the top of the tin. She gazed ahead until the lights on the opposite shore began to dissolve in her tired eyes. She took her heart medication. In bed, covered with two blankets, before drifting off to sleep, she felt a strong, brief bout of joy. She rejoiced that she is still able, that she is not dependent on anyone, not even her son Mikołaj. One tiny flicker under her closed eyelid.

She dreams that she is the nun from Olga Boznańska's painting. She is walking along the beach, along the seashore. The sea is rough and cold, and her shoes and the edge of her gown are soiled by wet sand. The beach is empty, the poles of breakwaters standing all black amidst the rolling waves. The wind would surely tear off her veil, but she has fixed it by wrapping a scarf around her head and under her chin. From time to time she glances at the horizon—the sea is brighter there, blurring as it touches the sky. Her eyes follow a tern flying by as it circles and stops on the wet wooden stilts jutting out of the sea. She does not recite the rosary, the large plastic beads on the cord hanging at her waist just tap one against the other, to the rhythm of her steps.

She leaves the beach, hikes up the cliff. The approach soon ends when the rocky walls of the gorge rise up on either side. There is a stream flowing through the middle and the boulders lying in its bed are framed by ice. She begins to climb again. On the steps carved into the stone, she is careful not to slip into the icy water. She turns her head, but the sea is no longer visible. The scent of rotten leaves and dampness lingers among the ever-narrowing walls of solid rock. Overhead, tall pine trees obscure the sky, their crowns moving. In the depths of the narrowing hollow, there is a small waterfall. The murmur of the water is steady and intense, the droplets settle on her face. Her gaze touches a niche carved in the rock, on the statue that has been placed there. It is made of stone, partly worn down, and turning black. In fact, there is only the shape of the figure that remains—the rain and humidity have worn away the face. The waterfall hisses and foams in the rock pool below. This is the end of the road, the end of everything.

She leans on a stone and stares at the splashing water. Her gaze encompasses the thrashing waves. She stretches her legs out, resting. Then, she closes her eyes and a steady hum fills her head. Water keeps flowing from the rock. The figure in the rock niche is silent.

The next day, she returns to the beach, but the weather deteriorates. The clouds grow larger and heavier, eventually they fill the entire sky. As she heads back to the guesthouse from the beach, a light rain begins. Soon it pours down. It rains for three hours. She reaches the guesthouse drenched and with cold feet. For a long while, back in the room, she rubs them dry and warms them with a thick towel. Finally, she comes down to have a late lunch.

Father Dariusz sits on a bench in front of the reception desk, looking out over the lagoon. As she approaches, she notes his profile.

The alabaster skin, still delicate despite the stubble, a finely defined chin, a small nose. Legs crossed. On the bench next to him is a Bible in a plastic cover.

Lamiel!—the image comes to her suddenly. She feels scared. Or Rastignac!—she imagines another image. She follows the Verbite priest's gaze. A white cruise ship rushes through the lagoon. In a few minutes, moving steadily, it will reach the harbour, then disappear behind the coastal trees. The water without shine, the opposite shore a dirty line, the white sky above it.

Later on, she packs her beach bag in her room. Her trek to the Camel's Hump begins with the steaming damp road. A few cars pass by. She walks briskly up the road with its peaks and dips. She observes the area to both sides. There should be a path somewhere—most likely on the right—that will lead to the top of the hill. Unfortunately, she is unable to find it—even when she thinks she can see a clearing, she dares not jump over the ditch and scramble up through the brambles. She sweats and feels little droplets form under her shirt and on her forehead, on her thighs. She has put on a lot of weight in recent years, but it does not bother her in her daily life. Now, however, she feels the extra pounds. She should have kept it in check after the heart attack. She has quarrelled with her son Mikołaj about this. He reproached her bitterly when they talked over the phone while he was in Jordan. And when they met in person, he gave her a wry look and recommended diets used by women in the Middle East. She responded with a gentle smile—my darling, I have no one but you, my son. She was so proud of her engineer, but his exhortations reminded her of the babbling two-year-old he'd once been, back when he was all hers.

She can see the amber jewel on her finger despite sweat dripping into her eyes. She wipes her forehead with a handkerchief and trudges on. The tarmac leads upwards, still with no path branching to the side, to the Camel's Hump. She cannot be sure she will find it. She keeps walking. Her thighs rub against each other. Unpleasant, a very unpleasant feeling, as a trickle of sweat runs down her back into her panties. Only Courbet's paintings displayed a similar boldness, legs open, the body rid of all shame, despite the mucus, the sweat, the dirt, the fatigue. Colours. In painting, she had always valued the washed out, subdued shades—the Chinese white, the brown ochre, these formed her palette, and now this asphalt and the absence of the path leading off up to the hill. She will never pour turpentine into a jar again. Anyway, the colours seem to have faded. Even trees by the roadside, despite summer being in full swing, sport some yellowing or yellow leaves. Fallen leaves are scattered on the road. She tramples over them, amazed that the short summer is about to die on these gentle hills of the Vistula Spit.

She thinks about Father Dariusz, about his paper-like complexion, his beautiful profile. The bout of malaria he lived through in the Congo must have changed the face of this Polish boy. He was probably from Mazovia or Masuria, and used to herd cows in the fields, and had a ruddy baby face that brought out smiles from his little sister, the one with grey eyes. They would turn quite blue as she was laughing. Then her brother, wearing his knee-high rubber boots, would pretend to threaten her with a cow's chain, and later, when the stove in the house was hot, they would eat potato slices which they baked by sticking them onto the iron door. The sister is now married to a farmer and is not doing well. Father Dariusz keeps sending her gifts. Sometimes he just gives her money, part of his earnings, not because she and her children are destitute in any way in their peasant house, but—in fact he has no idea why he does that. Maybe to commemorate that shared potato baking. Slices that tasted so good with salt and a sprinkle of black pepper. Father Dariusz must have contracted that terrible disease just looking at the murky waters of the Congo River. The climate there is unfavourable for fair-skinned people, really tough. Only a select few can adapt, and among those even fewer remain as they were before. She used to read a lot about Africa, in books from her father's little library—she remembers there was a bookcase with green curtains. Her father's dream was to go to Africa one day—the dream of a young pre-war boy. Following the war, he would just buy books, lie down on the sofa after work, and read them aloud to her, then he would give the books to her. Later she would choose them herself from the bookcase. You had to pull the woven string to open its curtains and reveal the interior, and its unique scent—the scent of anxiety and a girl's helplessness when faced with the knowledge, experience, and memories stored on those shelves.

Enough of this road. She turns into the first forest clearing she notices, climbs up from the ditch and then among the trees, and looks for signs of a path. Maybe there used to be a path, or maybe she will reach the summit by a different route, preferably an easier one. Under her feet, needles and pinecones—she glances up and, between the pine tops, sees the whitewashed blue sky. She will know when she reaches the summit. To one side, there will be a view over the lagoon, to the other, the sea. But now she needs to rest. She chooses a moss-covered plain, sits down. She is content.

She looks around to see if there are any spiders nearby. Then she lies down, tucks her bag under her head. A few moments later she hears the sound of the sea.

She dreams and in the dream, she sees Father Dariusz. The dream is very clear. He is dressed in a golden chasuble, its disconcerting shimmer emphasises the priest's sickly features. He is standing by the pulpit—it may be the chapel in their guesthouse. She hears his words, and, at first, is afraid she won't understand, but then his sentences get through to her without any problem. Father Dariusz speaks with a gentle, caressing voice. She listens: 'Schmergrube was a prosperous village located on the shore of our Spit. It was inhabited by a dozen or so families. The fathers were fishermen and went fishing every day in their sturdy boats. The sea was usually kind to them and they returned with nets full of cod, flounder, and eel. Their wives and children would wait for them on the seashore and help clean the nets. They lived in wooden houses with straw and rush roofs. The women were, by tradition, homemakers and weavers. A quiet village. Every Sunday, the whole community gathered in the brick Protestant church and the pastor would preach. He spoke beautifully about the Lord Jesus walking on the waves, about the miraculous catch, about how the apostles, after the resurrection, recognised the Lord when He baked fish in the fire. The interior of the church was whitewashed and the simple wooden pews were made of pine. The tablecloth on the Scripture table was also snow-white. The whole village was marked by such cleanliness. The Prince Elector once passed it on his way and was surprised to see that all the little girls had their hair braided and the boys' faces were clean.

"Dearly beloved," continued Father Dariusz, "let us ask ourselves: would we ever want to live in a village like this, in Schmergrube under the sand? That is—in a place between the lagoon and the sea, where we rest today, where we go to the beach and bathe in the sea? Thank God we can enjoy beautiful weather, and I wish to all the guests of our guesthouse that such weather continues for the rest of their stay. I now wish to briefly share with you a story that happened to me twenty years ago, here, in this very place, in the same guesthouse, which of course was not as luxurious as it is today, and I was a young priest just recently returned from Congo. I met a lady here—she stayed in the room opposite mine. We were neighbours. She was a very dignified person—she painted, read poetry, and during shared meals we talked about the news. We exchanged views on films, books, exhibitions. There was something about her that made me reflect on who I am, my life choice, the priesthood. Today, after all these years, I cannot quite explain who she had become for me during our short sojourn by the sea. Her subtlety was very different from what I faced in my daily life, both at home and during missionary work. The simple, stable work of a priest, marked by no ups and no particular downs, day after day, month after month—and then, suddenly, this woman, a pause in all of this, a frozen frame, life coming to a halt. And I was then, I should add, very ill, a fact I tried to withhold from my superiors. I did not want to get treatment or stay in a hospital. I trusted that the bouts of fever I experienced almost every night would eventually subside. This did indeed happen, but it took many weeks. As for the woman in the room opposite mine, I very much wished I could, on those sleepless nights, knock on her door and continue chatting, share who I was at the time, and look out over the lagoon together—from her window you could see it. I am sure that in the distance, you could also see the outline of the cathedral towers, out there, on the other shore.

"I used to pace the corridor, stroll along the beach at night, wander in the dark woods, listen in, not knowing what I was supposed to hear, and when I returned to my room, I tried to imagine the old woman, sleeping across the corridor, as she had looked many years ago, with her palette and her easel, setting out to paint outdoors, capturing her first impressions, the streaks shifting, imagined. I wondered what her hair might have been like, her hands, what was in her gaze at the time. I also prayed, of course. To understand. Myself, and perhaps also the world in which I found myself, to which God had sent me.

"This lady painter is long gone, but I know for sure that she found her way into the Schmergrube, that she fell in love with that place—just like she had with our village, which she used to visit with her son—and she decided to stay. She is even painting again. Life in the village is still very peaceful. It has a steady rhythm, in tune with the sea waves. The fisherfolk go out to fish, then return. As always, flocks of seagulls keep them company in the sea, and, in the harbour, groups of children. Every Sunday, people gather in the half-timbered church. They hold services. Such tranquillity is conducive to artistic work, and I see my long-time acquaintance lounging on the hot sand all day, taking out her sketchbook every now and then, so that they emerge on a white sheet of paper—the sea, the sand, and the sky."

WHITE WEEK

She turns her head. The evening city skyline, all in greys and patches of light, keeps moving past the train window. The river is dark, reflecting the colourful streaks of illuminated bridges, brush strokes of cinnabar and gold all over the left bank. That is the view as the train pulls onto the bridge: the eye resting first on the Teacher's Union building, then on the two towers of the Church of the Holy Cross and the Holy Trinity lighthouse. Then the red roofs of Krakowskie Przedmieście, the Grand Theatre cube, the Bristol Hotel all lit up, and then the clock tower of the Royal Castle and the last two specks: the dome of the Sisters of the Sacrament monastery and the Gothic tower of the Church of the Visitation of the Blessed Virgin Mary in the New Town.

She looks through the glass at the fleeing city but can only see the small figure of her mother standing in a church pew, her blue eyes almost completely faded, and an ash-grey raincoat with a belt, though it was warm. May weather. Elderberries in bloom, huge flowers piled on chestnut trees, though it had rained for two days, cooling the air down. Fortunately, on the day of the Mass ordered for her father, the sun had been shining since morning.

The church had been festive. She and her mother had both completely forgotten that it was white week, even though they had been here a year ago too, standing in the same place, in the same row of pews on the left, perhaps a little closer to the main altar. "Only days and nights may appear long; the years always pass quickly." Who said that? Who wrote that? Where did she read it?

Her mother stood silently, frail. She did not respond to the priest's calls, did not join in the song. Did she pray? Once, both the mother and the daughter had been Catholics, and the mother used to vehemently oppose her daughter's refusal to go to religion classes. "It is more important than school and all your interests!" she would cry out.

As she looks out at Warsaw sprawled over the left bank of the river, she recalls her mother's screaming. The sky is turning red in the east, then trees obscure it all, and the train takes a turn, stopping at the National Stadium. In the past, in May, they used to walk to the chapel in the neighbouring yard to recite the Litany of Loretto in the company of other women. Mother Most Admirable, Mother of Good Counsel, Virgin Most Prudent, Mirror of Justice . . .

Every year, her mother requested a Mass for her father's soul on the anniversary of his death, the 9th of May. A year ago, the white week children were few and far between with only ten girls, and the same number of boys. The pandemic forced their division into small groups. She recalled that it made her sad, so few children receiving their first communion. She knew it was only one of the groups, that there was another, but still—it was depressing.

This year was different. The children stood in several rows, the altar was decorated with white calla lilies. Their fragrance permeated the church, blending with the May breeze wafting through the constantly opening door. Some parents arrived late, after work, to pray with their daughter or son. Some carried laptop cases, having come straight from the office.

How about her white week? Several photos survived. In one of them, she is standing in her white dress in the courtyard, perhaps on her way to the church on Chłodna Street. You can see the benches, and trees that used to grow in the middle of the lawns. Next to her, there is Kasia and her little brother Paweł, who later became a priest. In the background, the block of flats where she and her parents used to live. The address was Krochmalna Street no 2.—a picture from a world that no longer exists, even though the building is still there, and the trees in the courtyard have grown tall. Her wreath was made of white daisies.

After she got divorced, she bought a flat in an outlying district. It was much cheaper; she saved a lot of money. Now, she commutes to the centre by high-speed commuter rail or suburban trains. They run frequently, and she has no problems getting to work. She still works a lot and lives on her own in a two-bedroom flat. Ania and her husband come to visit from Paris from time to time. There are no grandchildren.

Before the plague, too, the elder were in bloom. They scented her walk as she came back home every day along the street perpendicular to the tracks. After the outbreak of the pandemic, everyone locked themselves in, and she worried about her mother. The disease affected the elderly the most. However, her mother endured this imposed solitary retreat very well and got vaccinated as soon as it was possible, then made sure she got the booster. And another one.

It was she who became ill. Fever, no sense of smell and taste; fortunately, she'd managed to get vaccinated before it happened. Her neighbour brought groceries for her, left the bags outside the door, and pressed the bell. The time when she was stuck at home dragged on and on. After she recovered, she worked remotely—meetings were held online. She did not enjoy it. She got fat and flabby, spent her days in sweatpants sitting at her computer, only putting makeup on for those online meetings, when she needed to smile, pretend everything was fine, although it was not.

It was then that she felt the magnitude of her love for her mother, the love she had mostly failed to express throughout her adult life. She was not effusive by nature, but as she watched the news about the death toll rising every day on the telly, she became her mother's little girl again, standing in her white dress in a church pew, folding her hands in white-knitted gloves. Looking back to see her mum among all the other mums. And her mum was there. She watched her daughter with pride and love. After all, she was the only one she had!

In the high-speed train carriage, she enjoys watching the children. Watching their faces. One morning, there was a mother with a little boy in a pram; the boy would not stop crying. It was impossible to calm him down. He was probably sick with a fever, that was what she thought. Now, following the start of another war, a lot of Ukrainian children travel on this route with their guardians. She has heard their names: Vova, Solomiya, Nadia, Ruslanka, uttered by mothers who took shelter here, fleeing Russian bombs. The children and mothers are nicely dressed. It is clear that it was those who are well-off who managed to flee the war in the first few weeks and make their way to Poland, while the poor ones stayed, falling prey to invading troops.

She never liked history. Cruel and complex, especially the history of her homeland. Poland has been unlucky, that was what her mother used to tell her, back when she was a little girl, under the communist regime, when all you could buy in a grocery shop was vinegar or mustard—nothing else was available. People would queue up in long lines to buy basic goods, and the authorities would explain that shortages were due to the nasty American politics.

Back then it was May too, and children received their First Holy Communion. That old world is now superimposed on the new one, her vision double, she sees it all—then and now. Her mother has changed, diminished. She has basically stopped speaking and communicates with her daughter through her eyes, blue-grey, faded. Her mother would prefer her to still be married to Romek, she liked him, and had even once tried to force her to reunite with her husband, but finally gave up. Later, everything calmed down, became still, like chestnut blossoms on a warm afternoon—just like today.

Her street smells of elderflower and pork chops, or maybe it is minced meat. A dog is barking from behind a fence. She passes the houses, all of them fenced, until she reaches a new building, erected on a vacant lot. It houses several families but is not as big as the block on Krochmalna Street no. 2 where she passed her childhood.

Her neighbours' daughter is wearing a wreath and a white dress; she is coming back home from the church. They meet and she looks into the girl's eyes. In there she catches a glimpse of white elderflowers, or is it daisies?

DEVENTER

In *The Rings of Saturn* by W. G. Sebald, Kacper comes across the following sentence: "De Jong told me that he had grown up on a sugar plantation near Surubaya and later, after studying at the Wageninger Agricultural College, continued the family tradition in a somewhat straitened fashion as a sugar-beet farmer in the Deventer area."

Kacper found the book at his aunt's house by chance. Now, as he sits in a car park inside his new Nissan Sunny, devouring sausage and bread rolls he brought from Poland, while the river flows by, its current grey-blue, he remembers a visit to Deventer, a city on the river IJssel, a few years back.

He had bought the red car in Enschede, then there was Deventer all those years ago. Something came to him—he could not quite put his finger on it—something to do with his time studying at the Catholic University of Lublin when he was a young man. It was funny, actually. Kacper guessed what it was about, but rejected all memories. The wife, the child, the job, munching on the sausage cured with juniper smoke, jaw moving steadily, mouth crammed with bread rolls. He had come to the Netherlands to buy this used gas-propelled passenger car.

Many, many years ago, Kacper had lived in Deventer. He used to walk the streets there, admire the towers of St. Nicholas Church, stop by the pillory, eat fried fish washed down with beer at the local tavern, and soak his feet in the IJssel. A light breeze blew from the river, but it could not dispel the stench from the tanneries nor the sweet and nauseating smell from the brewery. He had met many people in Deventer—they used to be very close to him.

Above all, Kacper could listen. He listened and talked. Florens was his guide. He became a friend and maybe it was that friendship that Kacper recalled now, sitting in the red Nissan parked by the river that flowed through the city. All these years later, he knows that Florens was his only friend. He has not yet made another. Florens, his figure in the dark alleys at dusk. He liked to take a walk after a day's work teaching his students. They would wander around the market square and then circle around it, walking in ever larger and larger rings of the streets that were Deventer. They would end up on the riverbank, just by the Grote Kerk, and continue talking, often until one or two in the morning.

Florens was a man with a drawn face and a smile that revealed dimples in his cheeks and fine wrinkles near his eyes. His whole figure, starting from his red hair—already thinning near his forehead—to his clogs, was a necessary part of the city's winding streets with its many alleys, courtyards, and merchant houses equipped with cranes for transporting goods. Florens smiled often and would at times laugh his head off. Florens, Florens, Florens . . . My Florens. Mine alone. How easy it is to suppress memories of someone when daily life makes it impossible to even glimpse at the sky, especially when it as grey as the sky above Deventer.

At the beginning of this journey, however, Kacper had found himself in Enschede. He'd walked through the quiet streets—he'd walked quite a stretch from the train station. Cyclists passed him by. He drank coffee at a petrol station. Benny, the car dealer, smiled and was friendly, offering him a bottle of Grolsch from a crate. They sat in his office, basking in the morning sunshine. The beer was cool.

Kacper almost immediately reached for his wallet, took the euro notes out, counted out the agreed amount, and handed it to Benny. No haggling because it was all arranged beforehand.

"I have got many customers, some from Lithuania, most from Africa. I saw you at the station as I was walking to work." The Dutchman had light hair and a beard. "Enschede is a quiet city, a good place to live."

Again Kacper retraced his path to the gas station and bought a full tank of petrol, but instead of heading towards the German border and home to his family, he drove to Deventer. He thought about Florens and the others only when he reached the riverside car park. The IJssel was quiet so he could not hear the current, even though he'd rolled down both side windows. He finished his meal and opened a can of Coke, also bought at the station. Florens.

A meeting. He could no longer remember if it was the last one. He was surprised he could still remember it so vividly. They were sitting at a table, tin beer mugs in front of them. A conversation. How old could Florens have been then? Thirty? Surely not older. But when he'd talked about the path that had brought him to Deventer, it was unbelievable how one could give up so much of oneself, all those things from youth, and still find so much peace and joy. It astonished Kacper; even today, he still does not fully understand, although he very much wishes he did. Florens talked about his studies in Prague, where he'd graduated with honours, and his return to the Netherlands, settling down in Utrecht. He would teach philosophy until midday, and in the evenings he would frequent pubs and brothels. His world. Theology in the morning, then to the taverns in the evenings, full of merchants and thieves enjoying their nighttime pleasures.

A candle standing in a wooden bowl had begun to smoke. As was his way, Florens rolled up his broad sleeves and clasped his hands together. They clinked glasses and drank. His friend's face—tired, exhausted. He did not get much sleep, nor did he want to, maybe he was unable to sleep. He taught classes all day, then advised his students. He arranged activities, arranged accommodation with families from Deventer, and at the end of the day he prepared for the classes he was to teach the next day. He never talked about it, but Kacper knew that Florens solved many family and personal issues faced by the group he had placed himself in charge of. He read a lot in the cathedral library, even though there were few people in the city more educated than Florens. He could spend hours talking about literature, about Jesus Christ, about painting.

Kacper envied Florens, how knowledgeable he was, how well-read and, above all, how everything he talked about with such vivacity was directly related to his own life—the cool mornings, the noontime, sunsets, and long nights in Deventer. No flaw, one heart—his heart—and the whole world. How had he still found time to listen to others?

He'd wanted to talk to Florens, wanted this constantly. And yet, their conversations often ended with prolonged silences. Silences partly made of the sounds of the daily bustle of the townspeople: the clatter of carts, the creak of domestic cranes, the shouts from workshops in the narrow streets, the murmur of the waste streaming down the gutter in the street, and the rain spitting out into the streets directly from the gutters above, with their monster head spouts.

These were different silences from the one that surrounded him now, in this red Nissan. He'd had to buy it. It would certainly come in handy—he would need to drive his daughter to her pre-school, to the mental health counselling centre. But fulfilling his parental responsibilities did not make Kacper feel any better. Why can't I be like Florens? Why didn't I follow the path Florens had set for himself and his brothers? Something had happened. After all, I was also well-read, knew the sermons Geert preached on Saturdays. Hadn't I lived together with the brothers in the house that Florens managed for us? And I loved them all. John, little Thomas, Gerard, Gerlach, and most of all—the master himself. His gentleness and humility made him a saint surrounded by the coarseness of life. Day after day. We studied and worked. Some of us transcribed books, others bound them, still others sewed shoes. No one asked for alms. And Florens? After all, he was a saint.

Sitting in the Nissan he bought for €3500, parked by the IJssel River, Kacper realized the importance of those days with his brothers and regretted that the memory had only caught up with him now. Too late, although he is still not asking for alms.

The deserted streets of Deventer this morning. Not a soul here. Warm air and the clear sky. At the end of September. Kacper is walking along the river, looking at it greedily, but he does not stop. He turns right, but he does not recognise anything although he had been here so many times before, had counted the townhouses, known their shades by heart, the hue of each cartouche. Now he does not recognise them. He has become a stranger. The doors and wooden shutters are closed, the shops shut, no cyclists in sight. No one knows where everyone has gone. Paved streets, the same old gutters, tiled roofs giving off red reflections of the sun's rays.

"Tell me, Florens, why are we so tormented with thoughts about the future? Can't we focus our efforts on the life that is happening right now?"

Life happening now. It slips away, fast as a frightened hare. Kacper wanted very much to forget Florens, Geert—all of them— that was why he left all those years ago, started a family far away, in a distant country, why he had started to struggle every day and every month. He thought that by forgetting he would be able to face everything, to face each day, that he would have what he had talked about back in the inn with his friend by a flickering candle. That even though he had fled like a rat, even in his rat life, somewhere far away, somewhere out of the way, all that was his in the past would thrive, would somehow fuse with his life now and help him work, bring up his children, pray—and endure each day, day after day.

The city is vacant. He walks down Smedenstraat and has no idea where he is supposed to go. After all, somewhere there is the house where the men had lived together, in a stinky backstreet, right next to the smithy and the slaughterhouse. It was little Thomas who would pour out the waste every morning. Florens had stayed in the shabbiest room on the top floor—in summer it got no air at all. Apart from a few books and some parchment pages covered with fine handwriting, folded in quartos lying on a low table, there was hardly anything in there, just a jug of water and a wooden cup, a clothes rack. The brother who swept all the rooms each day had nothing to move around. The mess reigned on the ground floor instead, in the scriptorium and the binding room, the floor inundated with scraps.

By the time he came across the book Thomas wrote, Kacper had already stayed in the madhouse twice, once for a short time, then a little longer. He was reading a lot at the time—it was recommended by a psychiatrist—a lady doctor who wore a white smock and red tights. Everyone in the hospital ogled her. But she did not treat them like men—they were merely patients who needed help sorting out their lives, and who were to be handed back over to their loved ones eventually, if they still had loved ones. The park next to the hospital was huge, with trees a hundred years old and a thick blanket of grass. Kacper would sit on the grass and read, what else was there to do? Newspapers, crossword puzzles, the medicine that made his head spin. There was a hag in a white dressing gown, always snotty—he looked at her with disgust. She wandered about in her worn-out slippers. She would stand by the same pine tree, and over and over, talk to it, long monologues, perhaps a confession, recounting many years of her life in the ordinary world. Whole decades of her life.

Kacper would snooze in his deck chair. She'd wake him up, mumble something, hold out her hand. She had ugly catheter marks on her forearm. He accepted the book, thanked her politely. She walked away to stand by her tree. Then a sparrow squatted on the edge of his deck chair, crooked its head, and chirped.

"Pretty little bird, what do you need, do you really like the likes of me?" The thought fluttered in his hazy mind.

It was quite amazing that little Thomas had grown so much. He would have expected Johannes to do so. What language! Concise, precise, very evocative, that imagined a soul living, suffering, and seeking the path. Thomas proceeded with a flawless vivisection, chapter after chapter, describing fears, misgivings, and paranoias. The world he despised and the world he loved in order to write. Two worlds—the central theme of reflection by little Thomas, the resident of a townhouse in Deventer, the one with green shutters. All interspersed with biblical visions.

Kacper read, enraptured, throughout his stay in the madhouse. The lady in red tights assumed it was a sign of recovery. The eye never has enough of seeing, nor the ear its fill of hearing, so I shall detach myself from liking visible things, I shall not listen to those who praise or criticise me. Very well, said the lady in the white frock, her legs in red tights, crossed, and how do you imagine your family life? And work? I have the necessary knowledge which I wish to apply not just for myself, for my own satisfaction, because that is what got me here. Her shoe nodded.

In Deventer, Thomas had clung to Johannes and Florens, the two dearest people he had. Thomas, a skinny blond boy with blue eyes and his hair always standing out on the back of his head in a permanent state of disarray. He had a habit of twirling the longer strands of his hair on the finger of his right hand whenever he was deep in thought or when he was saying something, especially to Florens. And he grimaced in a funny way.

Florens expected a lot. Probably most from himself. I remember that once, in March, we feared for his life. He hardly ate any food, he only drank water and chewed on dry bread while lying prostrate on the church floor for hours, then in his room. The doctors said he had convulsions. Thomas was frightened, but it all somehow passed. The little one was afraid because he loved Florens—we all loved him. We listened to him, trusted him, because we believed that this man would lead us somewhere, far enough that when it was time for us to part ways, we would no longer need a master but would manage on our own, even without Johannes. And Thomas did, he managed brilliantly, which means he was right on track. He wrote a book that people are still reading, even in the madhouse.

Kacper wondered if this car would last. It was supposedly five years old. Benny assured him it was all fine. It ran on gas and was thus cheaper to use, only the tank had a different inlet than the national standard, and so a brass adapter would be necessary. There was a sticker featuring a simple figure of a fish on the boot, a memento from the former car owners. He asked the dealer what it meant, although he knew full well it was the sign used by early Christians. He was curious what the dealer's answer would be.

"The Reformation symbol," said Benny, adding that it could easily be removed, no problem; he gestured how. Kacper refused.

Finally, an open joint in the dead pre-noon Deventer. Sitting at the table in the corner of the garden, Kacper ordered coffee with milk and a small Grolsch, then stared mindlessly at the polished cobblestones of the street. How many times had he walked this way with Florens, with the others? How many times had he walked down this very street in despair, having listened to Geert's sermon in the church at the market square, and how many times had he thought he was one of the eternally damned, all hope lost? Today, he just swayed carelessly, drank his coffee, took a swig of beer. It was refreshing. How much of it remained: of Deventer, of lifelong friendships with Florens, Johannes, and Thomas? He had not made such friends since, though the book by little Thomas that he read in the psychiatric ward argued it was still possible to be faithful to pure impulses of the spirit, even on Sulpiride and Clomethiazole. Were they pure impulses of the spirit or the soul?

Florens had certainly known the answer—he'd known answers to many questions. He probably knew everything. He'd read the Bible and the commentaries, had written some himself, and knew the four Gospels by heart, in Greek.

Kacper did envy Florens his abilities because he could hardly read in Latin, though he had learnt a few adages. Years later he was still reciting them in the corridor of the madhouse, while the nurse dispensing medication gave him a radiant smile. When he was locked up the second time, the woman who had given him Thomas's book was no longer there. He'd never found out what happened to her. His second time began innocently enough, he'd read about a demon in Descartes, one that operated within or without, but most likely within. He looked up at the ceiling, at the mould that had grown in the corner of the room. He had long wanted to wipe it off, spray it with disinfectant. It was there that the demon materialised, he'd felt its physical presence and was frightened that it was about to possess him, that he'd need to follow its every command, to kill, to rape, to cut himself with a razor blade or a knife, to gouge out his own eye.

Deventer was once a bustling town with numerous boats that carried goods down the IJssel River. Its taverns were crowded with merchants, pilgrims, soldiers, prostitutes, thieves, the harbour and cellars infested with rats. Its market stalls filled with a throng of people from the surrounding villages, farmers, local craftsmen, floggers, and nuns in Franciscan habits and in the white ones worn by Dominican friars. It was the people who made up the times, the era. The time depended upon them. Tell me now, Florens, Geert, and you two, Thomas and Johannes. Tell me again about the time in which we lived, which we co-created with our conversations, prayers, and walks in the town of Deventer. Florens, you used to speak so beautifully of our Saviour. Tell me about yourself, who were you really, my brother? Sprinkle some ash on your palm, clench your fist. When the inside of your palm becomes humid, open it and read the pattern that is written there, perhaps you will then tell me about the time that has drifted away, along with the religion and honour closest to the human heart, quite like the sound of bells that spoke more clearly to people in the past, setting the rhythm of every heart. Month after month, year after year, quietly the centuries pass and the IJssel flows leisurely. Is there a special purpose to it, like the deadly air that haunted Deventer from time to time, killing people off, often whole families, whole neighbourhoods? Back then, no one asked about it. We lived. In all likelihood, the truth about the world trickled down along with the waste that little Thomas poured into the gutter every day, it loomed under the Cathedral's vaulted ceiling, in the cloisters populated by beggars, in the sound of the lepers' bells announcing their arrival. It was there, and we were all aware of it. The gleam of polished armour, of weapons, proudly wielded as the army marched through the narrow streets of Deventer. Swords, pikes, halberds, flails. Armoured mounts. Florens hated armed men, would mumble under his breath during military parades, and hide by the river or deep in the shaded arcades.

A now deserted restaurant in Deventer. Kacper sits in the arcade. A few more sips of Grolsch and he will have to drive the Nissan, to go back. Sin, transgression, damnation—so many unfathomable things—only Florens could illuminate them. Well, certainly Geert could too. He himself could not, he'd never been able to do it, not even now.

He looked up at the sky, at the white clouds slowly drifting in. It looked like it would rain. Rain again. He thought that even in the madhouse he was better off than here, at least he did not miss his life in Deventer, everything was neutral. He was not afraid of anything. Fear could be treated with a pill. Once, during Geert's sermon in the parish church, Kacper couldn't stop trembling; it continued for a long time. They all trembled, as if they caught it from Kacper. They were silent. They walked quickly along the night streets to the river, to their spot. Lit by the moonlight, the townhouses glistened like porcelain. Little Thomas sobbed, but Johannes only quickened his step and lowered his head.

They sat down. Johannes, a tall wiry boy born somewhere near Cologne, and next to him a little brother who had recently left his family home. Florens spread his leather kaftan on the ground and sat on it. Gerard and Gerlach, inseparable friends, trying their hand at the literary craft, encouraged by Florens, were with them that night. They wrote at night and bound manuscripts during the day. Gerlach, in particular, was a very skilled bookbinder.

Kacper gazed intently at the small man, the part and parcel of the very landscape of this town on the banks of the IJssel River, always brimming with energy, a tireless organiser of their lives, erudite. Everyone was waiting for him to speak. *Speak up, man!* Just a few minutes ago, Geert was denouncing them, calling for a complete change of life, roaring about laziness, the propensity for sensual pleasures, self-importance, lack of true love. He was so evocative that at the most solemn moments of the sermon, loud sobs and groans resounded in the church, several women even fainted. Geert promised everyone a shiny stone, given to the one who conquers and overcomes sin. A shining stone. Candles burned on the altar, torches on the walls, and a swirling darkness enveloped the vault. Geert, the fiery preacher from Deventer, silently stepped down from the pulpit and knelt before the main altar.

The river flowed in the darkness of the night. The city was asleep. Florens was still silent, so they were also silent. Thomas calmed down, Johannes put his arm around him. We listened to the noise of the IJssel. We had never been this close before, never as close after that. There are moments like this, never to recur.

Kacper did not worry about the Nissan. In fact, he forgot all about the car. He drank his beer, paid, and wandered off. He wanted to drive back overnight, in the dark, and to sleep in a car park in Germany, then reach home the next afternoon. Sleep again. The tank was full. He planned to fill it up once more near Hanover and once again when he crossed the Polish border. All supposedly planned, he hadn't come here to wander about, his goal was clear, and he had already achieved it. Kacper felt indifferent to it all, and there was something more—this was no longer his town, the life he had led here for so many years, his joys and sorrows, his work, his illness, all this—life—had obscured Florens, Thomas, Geert, and the others from him. He was surprised that they were no longer here, that Deventer could have changed so much, but he also knew, in his spirit, that he could not possibly meet any of them here. He had no idea where they had gone, but he felt that none of them would ever cross paths with him, that he would keep missing them. The closed shutters, the clean streets, the shop windows squeaky clean, the sun colouring the neatly laid roof tiles.

And that long ago night by the IJssel River, Florens had started laughing softly. Then he was laughing his head off, patting Johannes on the back. Everyone relaxed. We started talking. Florens thought that our melancholy was the right way to find the shining stone, that we were likely not just looking for ourselves in everything. That was what Geert meant. That was why Florens rejoiced. Florens, how good it was to know that you were there, watching over the adventures of every soul. Just you, dear man, and no one else. Back then, we all thought it would stay like this forever, that the world would never claim Johannes, his blond brother, Gerlach, or Gerard, that it would not claim the taciturn and timid Kacper. But the world was close by, in the gutter, reflected in the eye of a rat, and heard in the creak of an open window, in the clatter of wooden clogs against the cobblestones. It lingered in the sunrise over the IJssel that we watched back then. Though not all of us, Thomas was fast asleep.

Wandering around Deventer again, Kacper tried to remember what day of the week it was. Must be Tuesday or Wednesday. He was exhausted by the long-haul bus journey to the Netherlands and needed to sleep. He knew he had to sleep in the car on his way back. Coffee didn't help at all, and the beer had made him hazy. If Florens were there, he would have had someone to walk towards, he would have gone to meet a long-lost friend, they would surely have talked again, as they used to: about contempt for profit and reward, about trusting in humans, about Geert's sermons, and the Great Schism. Above all, about freedom, the only freedom there is—freedom from oneself. And about the shining stone.

Yet the town is still pretty, it soothes the nerves. The streets gently turn towards the market square, each townhouse manicured, painted in different colours. The sky above certainly remembers Florens and the others who walked through the backstreets so relentlessly, who sat by the IJssel, worked, lived, and were probably at home here. Even newcomers from the areas close by, like Thomas and Johannes, or further afield, like Kacper felt at home. They were free. Deventer was Kapcer's Arcadia, and it was worth popping in after all this time. And the madhouse was hell, he would like to efface all memory of it, but he cannot—the ugly paint in the corridor, grey oil paint with a sheen, at times the memories just appear; the toilets full of cigarette smoke and glass shards and water on the floor, cigarette stubs floating in it; a rag in a bucket; clotted blood on a towel that hangs on a wooden rack behind the door in the nurses' office; the window bars painted white. Only the park was different—green, surrounded by a tall wall. Whole patches of plaster crumbled away.

Kacper is in the market square and heading towards the Waag. There's a town museum there now. He should have a look. Maybe they keep things from the old days, though he does not expect anything spectacular. He looks up and sees the the stairs lead to two turrets. He has no memory of this place at all, but maybe it looked different when Florens was here. He has forgotten so much—his illness has wiped out some of his memory, and he was on psychiatric medication for months on end. If it hadn't been for the red car, he wouldn't have remembered Deventer, and wouldn't have come back here at all.

Later, after he forgets about this trip, that passage in the *Rings of Saturn* will guide him back to these very memories—memories of the trip to buy the car, the car that is leading him back to Florens after all these years. A complete circle, the snake devouring its own tail, though Kacper's mind could become even more unhinged, circling to a relapse of schizoid anxiety that will force him to take large doses of medication again. Florens, will you help me, my dear brother? I call upon you, for life is tough without you. Although not too bad, after all, I am back at work, the therapy has been successful. My wife and mother-in-law whisper:

"Mental state—very good."

And they make sure the news reached everyone.

The brick façade of the building is nearly pink, and there is a massive gate that leads into this historic structure. It is arranged in a modern fashion using plastic, metal, and glass. There is a lady at the reception desk, and next to her is a tall, grey-haired gentleman. There are no visitors. Kacper may be the only one that wishes to see the museum of Deventer's history. In the display case, there are colourful folders, key rings, stamps, postcards, and fridge magnets. He will need to chat to the man and woman a bit because he has no idea about the collections or where to start the tour. He introduces himself, says that this is his first visit but that he has heard of Deventer, that he has just bought a car from a dealer in Enschede, that he comes from Poland, and then, as he continues his incoherent speech, he mentions Florens, Geert, and the parish church.

The elderly gentleman smiles.

"They are both here, Florens and Geert. On the first floor."

Kacper buys a ticket. The gentleman continues to smile and invites him to take the elevator. They go to the first floor, then immediately to a display case with a glass box: two toothless skulls, side by side, resting on faded blue satin. Behind them, tibias carefully tied together with a satin ribbon.

"Here they are. They were kept in a church, but now they are in a museum." The gentleman walks away and leaves Kapcer be.

Geert and Florens, the master and his student. Finally, their souls can hold endless disputes, their eye sockets gaze into a softly lit and air-conditioned eternity.

"Florens! Florens, it really is you!" Kacper rejoices. Then he falls silent—Geert is here as well. He has a subtle mind, as indicated by the noble, arched forehead. Back then, Kacper barely talked to Geert, though he would listen to his sermons in church, and sometimes Geert would join them in their spot by the IJssel River, but Kacper never had the audacity to talk to him privately because he was such a highly revered man.

"You could have approached me, I even encouraged you to do so, once, don't you remember?" Geert is the first to break the silence.

Kacper feels a ray of sunshine breaking through the glass pane of the museum window, warming his heart. It stirs up playful reflections in Geert's eye sockets. Silence. Is anyone else in the room? Silence. Kacper is afraid that when he turns away from the display case that holds the skulls, they will not speak again. There is blue satin in the background of the tibias, the backdrop of the miniature setting of the reliquary that has been removed from the church.

"It is good to see you again, Kacper," Florens smiles. "After so many years! Our own Kacper."

"I have never forgotten," Kacper lies.

"I know what happened to you. I know about everyone who lived in that house in Deventer—I have been in the loop. I also know about those who succeeded us. Right, Geert?"

His neighbour's skull remains silent. Perhaps Geert is thinking about the sermon he is to preach for Kacper's sake, what to say to him, before he leaves on his long journey to Poland, in the red Nissan car.

"Tell me, Florens, will I ever recover?" the visitor blurts out.

Geert moves his toothless jaws and replies: "Does it really seem so important to you?"

"Geert, have pity, I have a child, a little child," Kacper whispers.

A frail little girl. White skin, sweaty forehead, a strand of hair stuck to it. Quiet, with a timid smile, everything seems to be fine, but she did not start school as she was supposed to. A lady in the counselling centre had tested her and found her to be ready, but at another centre they told us she is not ready, which everyone could see, by the way. None of the ladies said when she might be ready to start. The child would sit at the yellow table all day, arranging cards or doodling in the margins of newspapers. "It is a genetic disorder that she got from me," Kacper blamed himself, and though his wife said nothing, he knew perfectly well that she thought likewise. "Mental state—very good."

Through the glass, Florens's skull begins to speak:

"Geert, come on, Kacper knows how soft your heart is."

Then Florens's skull turns to Kacper: "The most important thing is that you have come, and we will certainly think of something. We have found a way out of many difficult situations before."

Kacper remembers that there were months in Deventer when they were all starving. There was food for one modest meal a day—mostly boiled lentils, porridge, or oatcakes, along with water or thin beer, brewed in the cellar by Gerlach. We were never wealthy, and never intended to get rich by doing something or serving someone.

Kacper asks, "Tell me, Geert, how much remains of who we were?"

"We are still," Geert rattles in response.

They did not manage to keep the townhouse in Deventer. Geert passed away first, then Florens exhausted himself—he did not need to be everywhere, to organise everything. He did not take care of himself and one week was enough to finish him off. The disciples dispersed, returned to their countries, starting lives they could afford. Some tried to continue together in small groups and lead a communal life in the cities, others got married and had children, and for some time, initially, remembered what they had once experienced in their spot by the IJssel River. They tried to remember, some tried hard. But over time, everyone forgot. The truth turned into legend and that was it.

Times changed and people did not wish to remember what Geert told them, or what Florens did, what purpose it had all served. No. Some considered it all to be a human whim, while others saw superstition, a fairy tale linked to the town on the IJssel River. But Geert and Florens—they were still here, first in their graves, then resting on the altar, then moved to the Waag, along with halberds, swords, and oil paintings slowly turning black. Now, they have reunited with Kacper.

"Tell me, Florens," Kacper insists, "why have I returned here? I was not looking for Geert, nor even for you, my dearest master. Florens."

"How should I know? I think you are looking for something, despite all the hardships that have befallen you since you left Deventer."

"Maybe . . ." Kacper says quietly.

Geert's skull is silent.

"But it is good to see you, Geert, and you Florens. I wish I could meet little Thomas, Johannes, Gerard, and Gerlach . . . I would ask Thomas to sign his book for me."

"The book is for us all," say Florens's remains. "We are all there, on every single page—and you, Kacper, are there too. That's why you keep reading these chapters, why they stay with you, because they are about you. Do you agree, Geert?"

Geert's skull is sunbathing. It must be very hot inside the glass box right now.

"You are healed, Kacper, do not fear anything," says Geert. "Go back to your country. Drive with care when on the motorway."

"Florens?" Kacper knows he has to go now. "Florens!"

In the marketplace in front of the Waag, it is sunny and warm. The white streaks of clouds have vanished. Streets seem more populated. Kacper notices the first cyclist. He is now thinking about his daughter, whether she would like Deventer—a town with colourful houses, narrow streets, and shaded alleys. Inhabited by people who hide from the view of strangers or perhaps leave early in the morning for work somewhere in other towns or in the fields, in greenhouses full of tulip flowers. As the sun sets, they return to their town, which greets them with arcades where they can sit, relax, and talk about how they passed another day. The years pass quickly, and so do the centuries. So much has changed in Deventer—Geert and Florens from the Waag museum know it all.

What would his little girl do here? Maybe she would jump rope or just hop, or ride a bike or a scooter, draw chalk hopscotch courts on the market square. She gets tired quickly. And she cannot drink anything cold once she's done playing. The IJssel keeps flowing. Kacper sees that it does as he looks at the river from the car park. He starts the car and slowly drives out of town. The Grote Kerk tower bids him farewell, as do the green sugar beet fields on both sides of the road with its flat expanse under the blue and pale-yellow sky with an occasional glimmer of a big industrial farm.

Kacper heads east. Past Hengelo he speeds up and turns on the radio.

"Fear nothing. Geert and I thank you for your visit. You will visit us in Deventer." Kacper hears Florens's voice for the last time, then there is music coming from the speakers.

WHEN IT RAINS

A strong gust of wind. The first raindrops hit the pavement. The corner of Jerusalem Avenue and Emilia Plater St. The wind gets stronger. People seek shelter under a canopy in front of the Marriott hotel. The rain intensifies, then becomes a downpour. A wall of water courses through the city, drenching the yellow trams and soaking people coming out of the underpass who run to find shelter or else go back down. The contours of the tenement houses blur and the dome of the Sts. Peter and Paul Church nearby is no longer visible. A woman crossing Nowogrodzka Street is wearing a light brown coat and sheltering herself from the rain with a pink umbrella.

Another strong gust, and the umbrella almost falls out of her hands. Running across the pavement in her light brown coat, the woman takes shelter in the arcade of the corner bank. The security guard standing there is smoking a cigarette, staring motionless at the rain-soaked street. He does not bother to turn his head towards the person who joins him so unexpectedly. He does not see a face with sagging, wrinkled cheeks, grey eyes with dark eye makeup, and a lipstick that is too pale. Her hair is ashen, glistening with raindrops. A passing car splashes water that hits the kerb.

At a table in the restaurant adjacent to the bank, the mood is different. The restaurant door opens and the rain-scented air comes into the room in waves, mixing with the smell of grilled meat and fish soup. The raindrops hitting the glass panes drown out the music, which is barely audible.

"You got him to publish all your books?"

"Only the second and the third one."

"And the first?"

The man stirs his cup with a teaspoon.

"That one was published by a small, private publishing house."

"Was that the novel where the female protagonist works as a secretary, things aren't going so well in her life, and she goes on holiday to Tuscany, where she meets . . ."

"I don't want to talk about it." The woman looks ahead, her eyes lined with black pencil. There is a calm certainty in that gaze, and curiosity as well. "It is raining cats and dogs!"

"Was that the book," the man insists, "where the male protagonist declares that Prince Poniatowski drowned in the Berezina River?"

"Why are you being malicious? What are you trying to achieve?" The woman shakes her hair, cut in a straight line above her shoulders. "That was a long time ago!"

The walls of the restaurant are covered by wooden panels whittled into a fish scale pattern. The waitress brings small candles, one for each table. The warmth of the flame and the grey surface of the water behind the glass pane—in an instant, the space is transformed into the cabin of a Spanish frigate, sunk centuries ago.

At another table, by the wall, there is a small man, a glass of whisky in front of him. His bald head nodding, he is clearly drunk. His crutches are leaning against the wall next to the table. The little man's short legs do not reach the floor. He takes a sip from his glass every now and then. He licks his lips with relish. He watches the room, particularly the two waitresses at the bar. Both are wearing short, tight skirts and long socks pulled up to their thighs.

The little man finishes his drink and beckons one of the girls.

"Pour me another one!" he says cheerfully and smiles. He has nice, even teeth.

"The same thing?"

"Yes, if you please. And tell me, why is it raining like this?"

"How should I know?" The girl's face expresses boredom. "On the radio, they said that it was going to rain all week."

After a while, she puts another shot in front of the man, and he chats her up again:

"Why are there so few people here today? Is it always like this?"

"It's the rain. In my place, in Tarnobrzeg . . ."

". . . is where the Vistula often overflows," the little man finishes her sentence and they both laugh.

The waitress glances towards the bar—she needs to go back and join her colleague—while the little man fondly dips his lips toward the amber liquid and takes a solid sip. His white receding hairline creases.

The window in the room where he lives, in a bungalow in a district far from the city centre, gives him a view of the weeds growing in the empty square across the street. Then there's a concrete fence, finally some buildings, suburban 'shittytowns,' as his late grandfather used to call them. The little man does not like the view, so whenever he can, he leaves his room, and wanders around the city, looking for adventures, looking for women. Late in the afternoon, he goes into restaurants like this one, accosts the waitresses, meets up with friends and buys them vodka. He rarely orders food, eating only a little, just a snack like herring in sour cream or Kashubian style, or sometimes some grilled chicken, which he chews for a long time. Every meal must be made complete with a chilled shot of Finlandia or Krupnik, vodka with honey, these two together are his favourite.

And after visiting his share of pubs in the city centre, the little man heads towards Mokotów, getting off the bus not far from the old Council of Ministers Office. The tips of his crutches tap against the pavement. He walks laboriously but persistently towards the subway, taking a long time to go down the stairs, holding on to the railing, then disappearing into the foul-smelling and draughty underground below the Crossroads Square.

"Darling, as a theorist of literature I cannot help but express my opinion on your writing. Critical opinion. I consider it my duty."

"How does it go? My worthy friend, grey are all theories, and green alone Life's golden tree or whatever. . . . You know it best, don't you?" the woman adjusts her chain necklace. The pendant has an infinity symbol studded with tiny luminous stones.

The man stares at it, and with an effort, he says:

"Modern creators who flee from theory will find in this stance their first Achilles's heel. Enrique Vila-Matas. And then there's that photo of you wearing a bikini by the swimming pool! Was it really necessary?"

"The publisher made me do it, and I wanted the book to sell well. Why, don't you like the photo?" the woman flashes a superior smile.

"To sell well!" he grunts with contempt and stirs his cup.

"Shall we order a hot apple pie with ice cream?" she says in that sweet voice of hers.

A thunderclap. The drumming of the rain against the glass panes intensifies. The waitress walks to the door and closes it, to prevent the rain from flooding the room. The downpour should pass soon—such summer storms tend to be brief, and besides, it is nice to sit inside a joint as the world outside gets deluged.

The little man orders another shot. His eyes light up with drunken playfulness and desire. Perhaps he is waiting for the rain to stop so he can move on. On such a day, he will call a cab, that is for sure. But right now, he watches as the door opens and an older woman in a light brown coat enters the room. The upper half of the coat is soaking wet. The pink umbrella has proven quite useless. The waitress approaches the newcomer and helps her remove the coat. The woman thanks her, smiles. She looks around and picks a table not far from the little man with crutches.

The man and the woman pause their conversation for a moment as two servings of hot apple pie appear on their table. The ice cream is vanilla flavoured. The man is dark-haired and has a round, slightly pouty face, with a three-day stubble. The partially unbuttoned shirt reveals grey chest hair. He looks like someone who hasn't spoken to anyone for a long time, like someone who has left his flat for the first time in days to meet someone he has not seen for quite a while. This is indeed the case, and he feels insecure, his sausage-like fingers slightly trembling as he lifts a spoonful of ice cream to his lips.

The wrinkles on the newcomer's face are almost invisible in the light given off by the flame on the table. She checks herself in the mirror, adjusts her hair, paints her lips with a bright shade of red. The waitress approaches, and the little man follows the girl's every move. Restless in his chair, he takes another sip. The old woman notices him, looks at him for a split second, then shifts her gaze to the crutches that lean against the wall.

"And I'm about to go into surgery and get taller!" he says with a taunt in his voice.

"Is that so!" she smiles at him.

"They will stretch my bones, so I'll be one metre fifty. Anyway, never mind . . ." the energy evaporates, and he no longer glances at the old lady.

He will go there, to the Crossroads Square, today, that's for sure. In the subway, there is a pub that looks like a corridor, with a bar on one side and an old sofa on the other. That is where the little man would sit until the morning, on the sofa where he has gotten cozy with women he has met on the street, buying them drinks, and drinking more vodka himself.

He once fell asleep and peed his trousers. The friendly bartender helped him take off his clothes and rinse them in the sink in the loo. But how was he supposed to get home without trousers? They were drying, and the little man drank more shots. It must have been four in the morning. Dawn as any other dawn. The taxi stopped at the 24/7 liquor shop, the man went in and then emerged with a bag full of beer bottles. His favourite, honey-flavoured. Or Somersby Apple. He would sometimes buy a whole pack and keep it in the toilet tank. To keep it cooler, perhaps?

It does not matter now whether he has any left at home, or whether he will order the cab driver to take him to his watering hole again in the early morning hours. There will be time for all that, but now as he looks drunkenly into the eyes of the woman at the neighbouring table, he is certain that he will soon be getting cozy in the underpass joint, then puke, and then wash it down with a shot of frozen Finlandia.

Her eyes are of indeterminate colour. Even more indeterminate in the twilight of the rain-drenched joint. They may be a bit grey, but there is also amber with a hint of graphite. The hands are positively wrinkled, with pronounced liver spots. The hands are now lifting the cup of tea. On one crooked finger she wears a ring with a red stone. The little man mumbles: "I am quite all right by the local standards."

The remark is uttered loudly, and the couple engrossed in their discussion about literature, devouring apple pie with ice cream, look towards the table where the little man is swaying. But soon they are back to minding their own business.

"So you think you are a writer?"

"I've long dreamed of being one. Even at university I filled notebook after notebook with my writing. I still do, but now I only write in the posh notebooks that I buy myself. Can you imagine?"

"You are bullshitting, can you imagine? But I used to love you very much."

The man's eyes now express his fear that his companion will get up and walk out into the rain. He hopes that she will stay and listen to the rest of his confession. It has been so long since he has spoken openly to anyone. She feigns surprise at this sudden verbal profanity but looks right back at him. She keeps listening.

"And this husband of yours, what do you get from him? Tell me, what is it? You have his name, and he is famous, which makes them publish anything you write, no matter how bad it is. Not because of you, how and what you write. It doesn't matter to them. They will take anything. Had you kept your maiden name, none of those fuckers would have published a single page of your work. Not one, do you understand? And you know what, they're all just doing you a disservice, and you don't deserve it . . ."

"I don't deserve it?" The woman shakes her head and then tucks her hair behind her ears. The man sitting at the table with her has often dreamed about this gesture.

"You could still learn to write—it's not beyond your reach at all . . ." his tone is soft, pleading.

"What are you talking about?" She laughs. "I authored three novels. I can . . ."

"'Ever since thought superseded style, everyone can write novels.' Camus."

"So what?"

"I wouldn't be saying all this, but I know you. I know you very well . . . That's why I say what I think. Do not think I am envious. Not anymore."

"All this is only possible here, in this country so full of inferiority complexes and envy. Do you know how people like me are referred to in the UK? People who write?"

"Well?" He looks up.

"Writer, that is it—just writer."

The windows after such a downpour are bound to be marked with streaks, and the pavement dries quickly, the water draining into the gullies. In this city, there is a special kind of light that is born after the rain—marked with the glow of a dimming day and the hope that a change is coming. Perhaps it has something to do with the smell of wet paving slabs, exhaust fumes, and the cool draft coming from the gates of the tenement houses that miraculously survive in this part of town.

The waitress, the one from Tarnobrzeg, opens the door again; they can breathe more freely. The old woman sips her tea, perhaps wondering if her brown coat has already dried, if she will be able to put it on without flinching, feeling the chill touch on her shoulder blades and arms. The little man has fallen asleep, his head resting on the tabletop, right next to his glass of whisky.

He dreams that he is standing at the bus stop by the National Museum, shouting obscenities at the people standing under the shelter:

People, you whores! The communists have taught you to only take, take, take! And now what? How about you now? Do you think, whore, that if Penderecki has a manor house, you deserve one too? Take, take, take, take! Why don't you say homeland, instead of 'country'? Why don't you say nation, instead of 'society'? Because the communists taught you that! Get to work, you fucking morons! You used to nap throughout your working hours and you think you can do so now? Understand, fool, that the communists are gone only on TV, but not in you. The communist regime is in you! And in you as well! And you! There is evil in all of you—you are evil, you are! Do you think, whore, that if Niemen had a yacht, you deserve a sailboat? Think again! You deserve nothing because all you've ever wanted is to take, take, take! The communists have taught you nothing, and do you know why? Because you only wanted to take and not to give, you learned to steal, to beg, to lie, to pit one against the others. And now what? What have you become? What does it look like for you now? Where have you landed? On your bare asses, that's where, because in this country, whores and thieves have always come out on top. That's the truth of the matter. She used to eat salceson with her fingers, and today she teaches good manners on TV. He used to stuff himself with pork chops in the Regional Committee's Bureau cafeteria, and today he advises on varieties of whisky and cigars. That's the kind of people you've bred as your elites—fucking losers. The Japanese emperor is visiting, and she has a flower tattooed on her tit; the Dalai Lama is visiting, and he's been pissed since this morning and eating dry bread because someone told him it helps you sober up. And she is pacing around like a cat with a full bladder trying to make sure the security guard doesn't bring him more booze. Your fucking elites! Are you so proud of yourselves? No pedestrian crossing in front of the school and the councillors don't give a shit, because there were more important matters to attend to in the urban area. But when a speeding lunatic killed a girl there, look, for fuck's sake, the money is suddenly there, they installed traffic lights and everyone is suddenly so fucking concerned. And don't fucking tell me it's always been like that. Always! Always! Is that all you can say? It was like that under the communists and it's like that now, because the communist regime is within you. You are the communist regime! But it doesn't have to be that way, people, it will change. Soon, you will be gone, your infamous past, I tell you that, the vicious dwarf. There will be no you, and you, there will be another state, there will be a homeland, not a country, there will be a nation, not a society, and then, very slowly, there will also be a reckoning with your past, you secret police whore. We will count—how many you murdered, how many you snitched on, how much you stole. Your secret service pals cannot protect you forever. It will come to an end—it is already coming to an end. That's the truth of the matter. You still have the villa you inherited from your communist criminal daddy, you are still barking that it is all yours, though it was taken away from innocent people, but soon we will come to get you too.

"Now, listen, another quote about you: Such is the fate of beings who, like ghosts, wander in the midst of this world. Żeromski."

"Nice, but not true. I am very grounded."

The man grimaces, perhaps a nervous tic. He drinks his coffee. It is cold.

"You're the only one who believes that to be true, even those assholes in marketing who pander to you at every opportunity know otherwise."

"You must really still be jealous of him. Aren't you over it yet?" The woman said it as if they were flirting. She smiles and shows her fine teeth.

The man looks at her for a moment, his fleshy lips not moving. They sit for a moment, as if still waiting for the end of the downpour, which has now passed.

"Jealous? Of him?" The man raises his voice slightly. "And who is he to me? Who? If you had seen him in Gardzienice back then. It was evening and we had run out of beer. I persuaded the bus driver to come with me to the nearby village. I wrapped up fifty bottles in a blanket, for everyone. I even remember what the brewery was called—Krotoszyn. I was happy that we'd made it, that we would sit down some more and talk. But that was not what happened. Because he and others like him, the ones you are now calling your— quote unquote—'dear friends,' started to protest: we don't know this brewery, it is certainly not a good one, beer from Krotoszyn, what is that, he only drinks Żywiec or Okocim. And he won't touch such a vile drink. It was then that I realised that he and I are fundamentally different, looking in a completely different direction, looking upwards and ahead, respectively. He is pursuing his goals and you are simply one of them. It seems to me that you don't deserve to be treated like this."

The man's voice trembles slightly as he speaks the last few words. The waitress looks towards the table where the little man is still asleep. She exchanges glances with her colleague and then with the bartender. Their intended action is pre-empted by the owner of the light brown coat. She pulls the sleeper gently by the sleeve.

"Wake up! Sir!" she says in a soft, gentle voice.

The little man lifts his head and stares ahead with no awareness. After a while, his eyes sparkle and he abruptly grabs the glass and drinks the rest of the alcohol.

"Please look out for yourself," he hears a voice next to him say.

The voice comes from deep down, from another world. It sounds alien in this place, as if it has come a long way and has just reached its destination. The little man listens to the sound of it for a while, then sways in his chair, perhaps musing. Finally, he speaks in a loud voice, one that everyone can hear:

"Madam, you are beautiful."

ST. JOSEPH FREINADEMETZ

It's nighttime and it's dark. I have moved the paper window back a bit, but even so, the stuffiness is unbearable. I can't sleep. My back hurts. Peasant huts reek of tallow and human waste. It is unavoidable. But it is nothing compared to the pain. I have not been able to sleep for several hours. The bed is hard, but that's something I got used to a long time ago. There is darkness creeping in from all corners of the chamber. Our Lord Saviour, have mercy on me, the priest in Shandong, have mercy on your Fu Shenfu. It was You, after all, who sent me here. I have grown old and I know, my crucified Lord, that I will stay here. At least the crickets are playing their music, and it is great indeed! The only music I can listen to here, travelling from village to village. Keep playing, my Chinese crickets, keep playing . . .

And me, what will become of me? I know, Lord, I will remain here until the very end. Among the Chinese who host me so kindly and who have already swindled me so many times, taken my money, shown me the wrong way, laughed at me, and once beat me till I bled. They still laugh at my long nose. I probably remind them of some kind of idol, maybe even Satan himself. 'Alien devil!' a child once called out after me as I was leaving their village.

I want to live and die with them. There is nothing else I can do.

The night is long. After a day of mule riding, the body must hurt. And it does. But when I rode up the hill today and looked ahead, I saw China. I saw the whole country. It is mine—the hills against the diluted blue, the trees as if cut out of paper, the rice fields all misty at dusk. Suddenly the wind blew and carried the smell of water, mud, and wet stones. That is a scent that brings about longing, always. Longing for my country, for my mother, my father, and my siblings. The green valley at the foot of the high mountains in Tyrol. Never again. I will have my homeland back in heaven—that is where I will see my hometown.

Now I have China, which has given me so much! Even the pain in my back is a gift, a Chinese gift, a torture inflicted on a stranger thrown from Europe into the depths of the East. But I am no longer a stranger. This is my country, so vast I don't even know where it ends. It begins here, in this village, where I shall celebrate the holy Mass tomorrow.

Their eyes. Dark as the bottom of a well. Sometimes the sky is reflected in them, the clouds flowing by. That is when they smile, but the gleam in their eyes remains dark nonetheless. A long time ago, still in seminary formation at Steyl, I read a book about how, just after America was discovered, people used to debate whether natives had immortal souls, whether they were the same people as us, Europeans. They debated in earnest. In the end, the church fathers agreed that the Saviour had suffered for the Indians and redeemed them as well. And the Chinese? When I arrived here, I was appalled by their pagan ways. Temples and deities with terrific faces, strange rituals on sacred mountains tops, where immortals were said to live. Colourful dragons roared terribly. I dreamt of them often. A devil's country through and through. What with the fireworks, the gunshots, the unbearable noise of countless festivals. Mottled costumes of unfamiliar cut, the painted faces of men and women. The incessant pulsation of an alien world. The smells. The stuffiness of Hong Kong's narrow alleys, where people never stopped cooking rice, fish, and various sea creatures I had never seen before. I came down with nausea and was sick. After a hot day, I would often wake up in a cold sweat, and outside—there was darkness. Just like today.

People smiling enigmatically, overly friendly, I didn't know them at all. I could not touch the soul of the Chinese. Human and sort of non-human. The Other. It was not enough for me to start wearing Chinese clothes, to learn the language, and to live among them. I was still not with, but beside, them. I needed time. Then I got to Shandong and it changed me. It was because of this place that I can now be thankful for China and the Chinese. I am at home. Wandering from village to village, throughout a vast country. The unfathomable plains over the flowing Huang He River, the moors, the terraced rice fields, the villages scattered among them. Misty hills. The more I felt averse to Chinese rituals, the more I bonded with the landscape. In the towns, there was squalor, perhaps even greater than in the countryside. The eyes of street urchins. At first, I did not know that so many of them were orphans. But I already knew that, for a Chinese person, it is the moment that counts. The one that is happening now, not the Last Judgement or the afterlife— they are not interested. Just the here and now, that is the most important thing. Just this very moment, this moment, as another may not be there. He is not interested in another one at all. And when I took care of the orphans, when we built the first shabby orphanage out of old planks, half decayed, managing to construct a roof, a small kitchen, and a toilet in the courtyard—when it was all there, already operational, that was when I first saw another face of the Chinese. The stretched, papery skin on the face, the slanted impenetrable eyes, the moist lips spouting quick words—suddenly it all became closer, they became closer. They were already looking at me differently, puzzled, surprised.

One day, a mandarin came to the orphanage. I knew people like him. Inaccessible, always with their entourage, following an incomprehensible ritual. But I had learnt it too, so when he came to visit—an event previously unimaginable—we followed a strict protocol. He was surprised, very surprised, to see a bunch of children playing and learning under the guidance of their Chinese tutors. I don't think he had ever seen anything like this before. Especially as some children were crippled, without legs, hands, or eyesight. He remained silent, smiling, slowly sipping his tea. We preach the gospel of Jesus Christ, I told him. He smiled once, more cryptically, or perhaps it was just a grimace on his porcelain face, and sipped again from his cup. The precious silk robes rustled. Then he kept helping us, sent carts full of rice a few times. Sometimes his help was simply to do no harm, to leave us alone. Lord, blessed be your name!

The night is really dark. Even the fireflies are gone. I think there's a lighter spot where the paper window is, but I can't see for sure. My back hurts a little less. Maybe there is water still left in the dish by the bed. I have to reach for it. Fu Shenfu's strength is waning. It is not a complaint. I stopped complaining a long time ago. I am here in China, and I am not going anywhere anymore, my fate is fulfilled, and the flower is slowly starting to die. The foreign devil will remain here. I am not afraid of anything, and the absence of fear is as beautiful as the heated forest glades I have often come across, riding the mule all day. The strange, huge, sweet-smelling flowers. The buzz of insects and the evening sun laying its soothing hand on everything. I kept celebrating Mass. For many years, I was accompanied by my guide, the blind Kangxi, he taught me the names of the plants whose scents he could unfailingly detect. But the people laughed at him too.

A sip of water—thank you, God Almighty, for this water. Now give me sleep! Maybe it will soon be morning. I cannot even pray. What a strange night, and a blessed one. Why shouldn't it be? After all, I'm in no danger, for I am here alone with my God. And there were sleepless nights when we kept awake for fear of the Boxers. They went from mission to mission, slaughtering and burning things down. Armed to the teeth, gangs of bullies in red turbans, sneering, grimacing yellow faces. They did not spare the Chinese who were with us, as if the cruel and audacious Guan Yu had descended from the heavens and was taking revenge for a wronged nation. We were sitting in a closed chapel, and all around us was a dark night from which an enemy with bared fangs was about to emerge. I prayed, for I knew that the Boxers were murdering out of despair, out of powerlessness and anger that strangers were ruling their country. The French, the English, the Germans, the Americans.

And then the Kaiser's brother himself came to visit us. That was when something snapped inside of me. In his presence, I started talking about Shandong and how the Germans, how all newcomers, were treating the natives. Hurting their pride, fuelling their rage, forcing them into bloody deeds. Is this how the white man's burden is to be carried to other continents? What are we, the missionaries, to do when the Kaiser orders the use of the 'armoured fist' in Shandong? There was consternation. The Kaiser's brother was silent, Governor von Truppel was silent, Bishop Anzer was silent. It was then, in a clear flash of grace, that I realised (previously it had only been a premonition) that I no longer belonged to Europe, that I had become Chinese and was on the side of those to whom I was preaching the good tidings. Immediately after the event, I was back on the mule, riding from village to village again. In this way, my destiny is fulfilled to this day. This is how it will be until the end.

I see a lighter rectangle. It is a window. So a new, blessed day is coming. In a little while, the birds should start their calls. As soon as it clears up more, I must open the breviary and carefully recite the entire liturgy of Morning Prayer. Without it, I could not live nor act as usual. The volumes of the breviary are kept in a carved case with a glass door. I never part with it. My back no longer hurts—the hope of the new day has killed the pain. The holy Mass to start the day, then teaching the catechumens, a handful of Chinese, who will come from several villages to gather here. Afterwards, I will eat rice with vegetables, and then I will need to get on the mule's back and move on. Is it true that the most beautiful fate in this world is to be a missionary? I still have some work to do before I get buried in the ground, but I know that I would like to remain Chinese even in paradise. When I am no longer here, one of them will pray: "*Please, tell me who the Chinese are / teach me how to cling to memory / Please tell me the greatness of this people / tell me gently, ever so gently.*"

ROMAN AND THE GIRL

Roman Dąbrowski cursed under his breath as the rubberised wheel of the forklift with which he was transferring multipacks of fizzy drinks into the shop came off the metal ramp. It took the boy much effort to fix it before he could shift the weight steadily again. He quickly forgot all about it, though, because he was thinking about the purpose for which he was now doing the work. The purpose. Ever since Renata was gone, Roman had often wondered about the purpose of his actions, even the smallest ones. Did he exist? Maybe he was not here at all, and if he was not here now, he might not be in the future, but could he be sure? He had no idea.

In the brightly lit interior, goods lay on their shelves. The space was divided by long racks packed with colourful packages. In the aisles, people cruised around doing their shopping. From time to time they came across a member of staff, usually girls wearing red aprons, trainee business management school students there on professional placement.

An old woman selling newspapers and books from behind a special wall has a good view of the whole business. She has a wrinkled face, grey hair tied up in a bun, and thick-rimmed glasses which distort her eyes. Her mind, however, is sharp—she counts money quickly, gives change, and asks the cash-desk staff to change notes into small change (especially in the morning, right after the store has been opened). She chats a bit with the cashiers and they tease each other a little. The fluorescent light brings out her artificial teeth.

Time passes the same way every day in the store. First the staff arrives, then the first customers come shopping, and, at the end of the day, the cash registers are counted. And finally, closing time. Under the barrel vault one can sometimes see pigeons and sparrows. They sit on the steel bars, their shit splattering down. The shop assistants and cashiers complain about the birds, but the only solution they have so far is to unload the goods from the trucks as quickly as possible, so that the large iron doors of the store's warehouse (where the generator is also hidden) remain open for as short a time as possible and the birds cannot fly in.

Circumstances vary, and no customer shopping here can foresee or grasp them. Unless, of course, they are the so-called regular customers and slowly become familiar with the ambience of the place: the smell of fresh bread at the stall next to the elderly newsagent lady, the coolness of the shelves sporting whole rows of beer bottles, the illuminated refrigerated meats and cheeses. The frozen food section, a secluded corner with dog and cat food. Stands crammed with packets of tea and coffee. Today, there is a discount on biscuits and mayonnaise. The least interesting part is the drinks section. Mostly multi-packs stacked on pallets, the unpleasant light reflecting off the plastic.

It was there that one might run into a girl with an allergic reaction on her face, the swelling so extensive that it distorted her features, making it unclear whether she was pretty or ugly. The red apron intensified that unpleasant impression. She kept hiding in between transparent cubes of fizzy and still-water multipacks, and when customers ventured in, she greeted them with a grimace caused by the unnatural appearance of her entire face. 'Renata Jaworska, a student,' it said on the badge pinned above her breast.

"She must be taking loads of antibiotics!" Roman Dąbrowski thought when he first came across Renata while looking for a cleaning lady. Someone had smashed a jar of tomato paste in the preserves department. They needed to mop the place. Roman was a sort of jack-of-all-trades in the store. He worked as a cashier, ending every transaction with the formula: "Thank you, have a nice day." He was also involved in the transportation of goods and took care of the girls from the trade school. Using the forklift, he brought the goods into the shop from the warehouse and then distributed them on the shelves. He was tall. Blond hair, mushroom haircut, and a decayed front tooth. Anyway, it may have been just a big amalgam filling, so visible because Roman often smiled.

The newsagent lady liked him. She joked good-naturedly that he should find himself a wife, a good wife, because after all, there were so many good girls, future wives, working in the store. "You keep on having your bachelor party," she grumbled. "Roman, my dear Roman, just look and see that the girls keep looking at you."

Roman would then flash his broad smile and, as he did every morning, hand over parcels of newspapers tied up with tape. Finally, he picked Renata Jaworska, the drink-section girl with the reddened face. She had the same family name as the former Miss Polonia. This marked a new period for the lovers under the store's vaulted ceiling.

Roman was seen leaning over Renata, while she was sitting at the cash register, patiently explaining all the steps to ring up the customers. The girl's face was burning red. Another time, someone saw them in the warehouse, they were standing, embracing each other among the pallets stacked with flour.

Life in the store went on. Photocell-controlled doors kept sliding open to let the customers in, buns were baked, the same homeless drunk begged in front of the entrance for someone to spare him some change. His white beard was dishevelled and the skin on his legs was red from scabies. No one knew why he was in the habit of putting plastic bags on both his hands. The apprentices were about to finish their placement. Roman Dąbrowski teased them, saying that they would all return to the store one day—as there was no place quite like it—and work under his guidance, even though the corporate site in charge of the store continues to increase its turnover year after year.

For the time being, however, only Renata Jaworska had been offered a permanent position. Everyone knew it was because of Roman, and they accepted it as normal. She was a good girl and he fell in love with her and landed her a job. She was still stuck in the same spot by the drinks, but the news was that she would soon be sitting at the cash register, to replace Monika who was going on maternity leave.

Renata and Roman's love seemed to be in no danger. They were planning to move in together, something Roman wanted to keep secret from some of the staff, above all the elderly newsagent lady. She would certainly not have approved and would have pushed for them to get married.

By autumn, Renata's face brightened a little and her complexion became noticeably healthier. She had by then been promoted to a cashier.

"Look, her 'I-don't-get-enough-of-it' pimples are going away, Roman has been doing a great job," sneered Agata from the meat stall.

However, after Christmas, Renata took more and more sick leave. First a week, then three weeks, and finally, she stopped coming to work altogether. The tiny community of the general store knew, as is always the case, that Renata was gravely ill and that it was some kind of blood disease. Roman Dąbrowski went to the hospital each day after work. He bought juice boxes for her from the store's warehouse. He got them at wholesale prices by settling directly with the supplier. He walked along the damp streets to the hospital where Renata was suffering, but first he stopped at the church. Its tarnished tower stood out sharply against the sky in this quarter of the city. Roman would sit down in a pew and stare into space in front of him and then, mustering his strength, he would leave.

The hospital building looked a bit like the general store, Roman kept pointing out cheerfully. It was there that he met Renata's parents. They were farmers and would come to visit their daughter, bringing money to bribe doctors and nurses. Their Skoda was the colour of the hospital walls—a mixture of muck, dirt, and rust. Her father would smoke three cigarettes (the brand name "Fajrant" meant "end of work") in the courtyard. Her mother would cry in the corridor. Roman was present for all of this, keeping his stoic calm, only occasionally smoking a cigarette with Renata's father, his hands trembling as he did. Apart from that, he did not show his pain.

Renata could no longer get out of bed. She became limp and shrivelled—wasting away, more and more, each month, a shadow of the former cash register employee. The hardest thing for Roman was to hide it from the staff at the store, but he didn't actually have to because a colleague kept visiting Renata and so the women had firsthand intel from her. He said nothing and they did not ask.

Today, the sun was shining for the first time in many days. It reflected off the wet roofs, water dripping from the gutters, and luminous sparkles danced in the puddles. Sparrows were bathing. Renata

Jaworska died at nine o'clock in the morning. Roman found out after work, from the head ward nurse. He visited Renata in the room where they kept the dead—the doctor said it was okay. Her parents were there, and he greeted them warmly. They sat on the chairs in the corridor. The mother was wailing. He went out into the courtyard with the old man. The father's eyes were red. They had a smoke.

"It was meant to be, apparently," Roman heard the father say. After that they talked no more.

At the store, the staff all chipped in to buy a funeral wreath at the open-air market nearby. Roman was the only one to attend the funeral, as it was held in her home village, so he took the wreath and travelled to the site by local bus. Then he walked along the road, avoiding pits filled with brackish water, looking at the houses topped with roofing paper, the messy yards, and the chickens roosting there. A few cars were parked outside the church and some mourners were standing by. He had not stopped by Renata's family home, where they had held an all-night vigil. He would not be able to look at her. Even at the hospital, after she passed away, she seemed alien to him, somehow very distant from his own Renata with her inflamed face, the store clerk in her apron. A different person altogether.

He threw a handful of earth on the coffin, then laid down the wreath. He did not join the traditional vodka drinking at the wake either. Instead, he dragged his feet back to the bus stop.

"The first and most basic rule is that if the manager is trying to screw you over, you screw him over, too. See, I worked very hard and what did I get? I'm telling you how it is. Where are you from? Where from? Ah . . . Well, at least you don't have to get your hands dirty with muck like we do. My son drives a forklift, too, in that big—what's its name?—well, in a warehouse . . . Do you want a drink? Have a shot, why not . . . You are young. The cherry liquor holds on fast. I drink two daily. I love the cherry liquor very much, it's like a wife to me. It is not easy for my son. It is tough for him, he has to work, he does not earn much. And so you've come from the funeral? I know them, I know them, I fucking know them all—the farmers, each bloody house, I could write a book about them, and it would be interesting, as life always is, a thousand pages thick. I knew Renata, yes I did. And who are you to her? Her husband? Not a husband? You're obviously an intelligent boy. And you, brother-in-law, you go away now, I ask you politely, fuck off, let me talk to this intelligent gentleman here, fuck off, I tell you! Here, have a sip of wine! Renata was a pretty girl, I remember everything, she used to take geese to graze by the river, had sex with the boys there, and what do you think, the rushes are thick, and they move all the time. They are all like that now, they fuck like cats. When I was young, it was different. And then, when she moved to the city, I don't know what she was up to. They are all the same. She worked in a store? Maybe she did, if you knew her, that is probably true. And also . . . And her father is, you know, a day labourer, a miser that is, like all of us here, but he used to be strong, there was no one quite as strong as him. And he was in prison for murder. The story went like this—there was a woman in his house, and then there was not. Dead. He never spoke about it. He spent a few years on the planet Venus and then came back and got himself a new woman. And that's how they live, the old bags, the Jaworski couple. And you, brother-in-law, don't bullshit me that the boy will be offended, I can see he is intelligent, and I'm telling the truth. But now if you excuse me . . . another sip.

"The bus will be here in a few minutes, but I'm not going, I have nowhere to go. What is your name? Roman? I knew one Roman, in the army—I too served in the army, I did, I spilled blood for all of you. You see? Three fingers are missing—a grenade ripped them apart, and so what? I live on, and when I have nothing to eat, you know what I do? I kill a chicken, pluck the feathers, put it in the pot, and it is fine for me. You know, Roman, I'm sorry, we were not on first-name terms, are you angry? You're not angry, right? Are you sure? I'm telling you, Roman, fuck me, things are so bad now, it's not good, but why am I telling you, you know for yourself, you live in the city, it's not good, it's worse than it used to be, right? I'll have another sip . . . And I tell you this—no regrets, do not regret anything, don't fucking cry, Roman, no, I don't regret anything, I keep living my life. Your Renata would have no regrets either, because she was a good girl, I used to know her, oh, she used to come here to the pond. The bus is coming, for fuck's sake. Get in, Roman, I wish you a good journey, come back sometime, me and my brother-in-law are always here and waiting for you, because you're an intelligent boy. A different person altogether."

REPEATED MISTAKES

She pulls on the leash. She is strong, stocky, although of medium size. A real mongrel, something like in *Peasant Coffin* by Gierymski, where the dog is curled up in a ball on the road in front of the cottage, indifferent to the owner's grief. Only mine does not have a tail. It is unclear what her story was, the bitch they named Carmen at the dog shelter. The woman who owned her died, that is all I know. She was a lonely old lady living on a farm, somewhere to the south of Lublin. The heirs noticed that there was a dog on the farm, left behind when its owner died.

The bitch was chained to a stake by the barn and was afraid of strangers. She is still afraid. She has begun to trust me, but she only comes within my arm's reach, and she avoids the other household members. She mostly hides in the kennel, except when it is time for a walk, then she comes out and starts to squeal.

So, we take a walk, our urban forest is turning green, though tentatively. The leaves are still small and the needles seem dirty after the winter. It is the end of a cold April. Another week, a week and a half, and the forest will have undergone a complete transformation. The dry needles and leaves will disappear under the green undergrowth, and the grass will grow where the plastic film from a four-pack of beer now lies, and the leaves will rustle above, big ones, maple, beech, and oak.

Carmen keeps wandering off the path, sniffing shrubs and clumps of dry brambles. Each time, I have to stop with her. I still keep her on a leash—she's been with us for just two months. She could get scared because of a madman on a motorbike speeding down Soldier Street, and how would we find her then? The phone number tag she has on her collar may be of no use. Besides, she would not let anyone approach her.

The path leads through the young forest. Furrows are still visible between the pine trees, shallow trenches from which the tightly planted trees later emerged. A dozen years ago, the town leaders planted a strip of forest along the busy road leading from Warsaw to Nieporęt and on to the Zegrze reservoir. We never go that far, of course. Together, Carmen and I visit the surrounding woods and groves. She is very keen to explore, especially as she used to be chained up all the time. The so-called chain dog.

"Dear Wojciech," Kazimierz told me on the phone a few days ago, when I told him about the dog and her story, "in our supposedly Catholic country, animals are treated badly and people are cruel."

Precisely, dear Kazimierz, that is what I am thinking as I walk the forest path on this cold and cloudy day. I value these phone calls we have because he speaks to me in a way that seems simple and ordinary. I remember a lot, it stays with me, somehow. We have been friends for a dozen or so years now.

It is good that it is not raining. I should be happy about it, just like I should be happy that a country mutt like my dog finally stopped being miserable and started a better life. Does she understand this? Probably not, not really, but she may sense something. There may be some recollection in her whimpering that rings out again and again in the forest.

The forest is a refuge. It became a home after the Polish manor houses were burned down during World War I and II, and the families who lived in them were displaced. Afterwards some of them were deported to Kazakhstan. The forest was also a refuge for the resistance fighters who hid there. One of the forest troop commanders in the Jata primal forest even took 'refuge,' *Ostoja* in Polish, as his *nom de guerre*. I went there many years ago to attend a forest Mass to commemorate the battle of Gręzówka—Ostoja, Jata, Gręzówka, I am reminded of everything as I pull on the leash, Carmen once again veering off the path. The forest is also a bleak place, where bad and cruel things happen. Winters spent in a forest dugout. It makes me sick just thinking about it, yet so many people shared that experience. The cold, the damp, the lice, the stale air. A short story by Tadeusz Różewicz recounts it. And one character dreams of seeing the sea at least once in his life. The sea? Potatoes with bits of fried pork lard are more like it!

I arrive at a lone oak tree. A small cross has been placed by it. Name, surname, male, 23 years old. A few candles. I know the story of a boy who used to wander this forest with beer in his hand. He kept coming here with beer. Eventually, he killed himself. Hung himself from this oak tree, here in the centre, admittedly the best spot, and a pretty tree, a dignified one. He took the truth about his miserable self to his grave. His true intentions, no one will know. And that is a very good thing. Let his death be the secret of the place.

The dog pricks up her ears. The silhouette of a jogger flashes in the distance. These joggers run to stay healthy, they take care of themselves, they want to live better and longer than their mothers and fathers. Dressed in synthetic bodysuits, they wear headphones, streaming in music as they run, or maybe the news, so they do not heed the place talking to them, so they cannot hear what the forest wishes to tell them. Nor do they hear the whirr of engines coming from Soldier Street. The city road was recently redesigned, with a wide strip of forest cleared for the purpose. It is now easier to drive, safer. We are still in a big city, after all, the biggest one in Poland. But, on the outskirts, some wilderness remains—the Kampinos Forest. It is on this side of the Vistula River, stretching out next to the city in a different direction from where I walk Carmen. Part of this forest where we walk is within the city limits, part without. Here people and dogs stroll by, roe deer and wild boar, and birds, mostly birds. They keep singing as we keep walking.

I wish I could let her off the leash. Let her run freely! It is still too early for that. Kasia, the lady who brought her to me from the shelter, told me that Carmen used to live under some old, corrugated sheet of fibre cement and planks put up against a barn wall—that was her shelter. A neighbour, who was supposed to care for the dog after her owner died, would throw in a handful of dog food every now and then, and bring her a blanket. He was a drinking man, so such negligence is no surprise. Eventually, the chain got so short from her circling the stake that she could not move.

"She chewed on the metal, which is why she doesn't have the front incisors, as you noticed."

We are now walking along a wide forest road and the leash gets tangled under the dog's feet. We need to buy an automatic retractable one, three metres long. How old can Carmen be? They said four. She could be five or six. On the right, about a hundred metres off the road, there is a large hut, with some old chairs set up outside, some rags hanging from the branches. Someone must live in here. I once thought about looking at it up close, this woodland hideout, now fully visible to those walking along the forest road. When it gets greener, the hut will disappear again. But why would I go there, what do I want to see? Someone else's misfortune? There are many such stories of desperate people nowadays, those silly TV shows recount them. I wonder if it has always been this way, or if it was technology that has led us to feel this unhealthy curiosity, which ultimately is just a way for corporations to make big money.

The bitch pricks up her ears again and raises her head. There is a man sitting on a pile of logs that have been felled and laid to the side. He supports his head with his hand, his fingers smeared with something. Carmen keeps her distance as much as she can, the rope stretched so I have to pull it. She looks at me, terrified. I look calmly at the man. Bald head, stubble on his cheeks, he wears denim that does not suit him at all. An empty yellow can of Tatra beer has been put upright between the logs. There is nothing left in that gaze of his. It seems to say that life itself—regardless if it is better or worse in a forest hideout or in a house with a fireplace—no longer matters. All that matters is fate: the birthright of every living being, from the woodpecker in the tree to the man dwelling in this hut.

Beyond the barrier, the view of Soldier Street. A two-lane road, with a cyclist path and a pedestrian lane on the side. Cars painted different colours, trucks, the straight stretch of road inciting mad-men to hold nighttime motorbike races. Heavy traffic now. Lots of cyclists as well. And joggers. Rollerblade riders. A bike like those in Amsterdam, a pink coat, a golden little backpack glistening in the sun, and a cascade of bright hair. She rides slowly, she does not want to get sweaty, she is heading for a meeting, she cannot get dirty. She is dignified as she presses onwards, though she cannot be more than sixteen.

I choose to walk along the cycling path, a wire fence between the cyclists and me. We walk on the forest grass and I let the dog sniff all she wants. I wish she could tell me about her early years: about the people she was with, whether her owner was good to her, about her neighbours, the drunkard who threw her a blanket. And how many puppies she has had and how many litters, because even though her nipples are partly obscured by the white fur on her belly, it is clear from how they sag that she had many litters. Was there a river by the village? Were there ponds or swathes of forest? Were there tall poles for the hop plants found across the region? These questions will remain unanswered. I can only imagine that maybe the village where she comes from is surrounded by deep forests where Jews hid during the war, where forest troops fought even after the war, the last of them mercilessly hunted down and shot in the back of their heads by our secret service police. I wonder, how were these people different from the SS officers? The only difference may have been nationality.

Carmen is a stupid name for this unfortunate dog.

"Dear Wojciech," I hear again the deep, calm voice of Kazimierz. "Don't ever forget that people are cruel, and that unfortunately evil is on top. It catches the eye. But the essential point, dear Wojciech, seems to me to be that literature cannot affirm evil. It is unthinkable to represent evil for the mere satisfaction of describing it. Instead, the point is to describe evil as evil. An attempt to oppose rather than to affirm it."

Literature in the forest. The words uttered by Kazimierz resonate in the spring air. This voice calms me down. Even the mere memory of it. The dog on her leash has triggered this avalanche of associations. There is a plastic bag hanging from a bush. The wind makes it crinkle and fly like some kind of flag, a symbol of the times, or maybe just of this area. Like the plastic bag swirling in the wind in *American Beauty*, the faking of something deep and sublime, a kind of transcendence, but fake. Pretending to mean something when, in fact, it means nothing. This bag is transparent and hangs proudly on a bush, even Carmen is not afraid of it and she tends to be afraid of everything, even the rustle of a windblown dry leaf on a sidewalk. But not the forest—she likes coming here, and whenever we walk towards the white and green barrier—the gate—she turns around and seems to grin cheerfully. I think she is happy then—she seems to be smiling at me. Her eyes sparkle and it seems that she is about to tell me all about herself. But is there really anything worth taking about? The farmer lady who used to beat her with a stick and made her sleep under the wooden planks, the chain biting at night—it is all gone for good, and we shall continue walking through the woods as they get greener and greener every week until autumn. And we will continue to come here in the winter, too, because where else would we go?

A little grove on the right, and we enter the forest again. Tall trees, and last year's oak and maple leaves on the ground. They are ashen in colour and soon they will be swallowed up by the greenery and decay, then ferns will burst forth and so will the tall cockspur, its blades razor-sharp, and the blueberries and hazel will turn green, as will the young trees that grow here side by side. And mushrooms, will there be any this year?

The very end of April has been cold this year. And rainy. Now, that the sun is out, things are getting cleaner, almost elegant. A dark green helicopter against the sky, from the military training ground in Wesoła. Carmen is getting restless again. A girl and a boy walk in front of us. He has a bag slung over his shoulder and seems to be explaining something as he leans towards the girl. Almost time for their A-levels, and they are walking through the woods, maybe discussing a maths assignment. He is clearly preoccupied, but perhaps it is she who excels in maths. Both become part of my walk with Carmen. The name is indeed moronic, but I decided against changing it because the dog was so miserable when she joined the family that she hid in the kennel and didn't come out for two days. I would force her out and take her on a leash to the garden, but she's not like that anymore. Sometimes she lies in front of the kennel and scans her surroundings.

My high school graduation. Thirty years ago, back then, under the communist regime, the time so distant to these two young people in front of us on the forest path. When I was nineteen, I felt the Stalinist times were equally distant. Perhaps I made a mistake. Right after I graduated from high school. Maybe I should have done something completely different, chosen a different direction, maybe I did not follow the right path among all those other forking paths, maybe I would have been wealthier today, more confident, not looking back as I am now. I would have met different people and not have wasted so many opportunities and so many years pursuing futile interests, reading meaningless texts, succumbing to meaningless passions, falling in love by mistake, and repeating that mistake over and over again. Such musings, of course, are pointless, but I suppose I can indulge myself a bit in this April, still-chilled forest. Nobody minds, though these are the musings of a loser. I have made many more mistakes, by the way, all unawares, with the deepest conviction that I was doing what should be done.

The blackbird's song. The eternal whistle. It has always sounded the same here. Even when this forest track was not yet here, when there were no humans in this forest. Or maybe it was planted by humans? You can never tell. "My understanding has always been a mistake. My heart's every deed, every act—missed the target. Everything always turned out differently than I had intended, foreseen, calculated. Everything happened differently than I had dreamed. Apart from my logical reasoning, everything else was awry, followed its own way. Out of the darkness a storm was falling over my field. Out of the darkness death was coming at me. Sometimes, way in the distance, the line of my dimension and drawing met with the line of another dimension, not mine—but far, at such an infinite distance, that I could only imagine seeing it happen. By then it was all the same to me. My triumph so invisible, so imperceptible, that it turned into a brief, little solitary half-smile, a point, as geometry experts would have it." Żeromski, he understood mistakes.

But I am not at all sad or unhappy. On the contrary. I do have a forest and a new, old dog. I do not resent God who sends a hailstorm that destroys the blackbird's nest, or the cat that hunts little squirrels and brings them back just for show. I am not so belligerent, so pompous as to flex and curse, swear or threaten . . . Cut myself, get a tattoo, chain myself to a tree. No human being could possibly invent such a forest and the blackbird that's in it, or that student couple. Such things are beyond human making. None of this can be a mistake, I think to myself without a thrill, as we approach the clay pit filled with water.

Shrivelled plants by the shore. The dog steps into the water but immediately backs away, only getting her front paws wet. Someone used to mine clay here; there was a brick factory down in Zielonka. Back in the 1950s, they made the bricks needed to rebuild the nearby city, which had been completely destroyed. The city has been rebuilt, but the water-filled pit remains. We are now walking along its high bank. The road turns into a path which forks by the grove of young trees. We should turn left, I think, and then go straight ahead. There is always this uncertainty, though I have walked this path many times before. A few dozen metres more and the monument becomes visible.

Kazimierz's voice resounds with experience, whole years of life: "Dear Wojciech, why do you think it cannot get any worse? It certainly can. The poet wrote that wise books have done little, and mad books turn the world upside down. Strong is the wrath of Zeus, powerless the groan of Christ."

The chestnut trees are not yet in bloom. Cold drafts of air pass between the tree trunks—I feel them on my cheeks. The dog keeps pulling me ahead. Wide head, large muzzle and nose, and pointed, light brown ears. She is all white around the muzzle and on the cheeks, with a white belly and paw tips. Black on her back, and, as they say in Mazovia, all in all, medium. And another important thing—no tail, what's left of it is a mere brown stump, which is sometimes in motion. You cannot really call it a tail though.

Or are we now walking through the woods out of spite? No, we are going for a reason, nature is waking up from winter, the dog is pulling the leash, the line is tightening. We are walking despite the still prevailing cold, the dead leaves scattered under the trees, the old pinecones trampled into the ground, the cold water in the clay pit. We simply walk because we like it. We go despite Kazimierz voicing his concerns about the fate of the world. I worry about the world too, but not now: I do not care about the past or the future, nor do I think about climate collapse or readership levels, or animal shelter conditions. All of this is incompatible with our moving through the forest, which is why Carmen and I are savouring this one moment we have been given, for free, right now. Can anyone take it away from us?

We approach the monument. It is tall, made partly of stones collected from the surrounding fields and the forest to commemorate an event that occurred on 11 November 1939, the first anniversary of independence from under German occupation. The scouts from Zielonka pasted leaflets with *The Oath* by Maria Konopnicka all over the area. The leaflets stayed in place for some time, but then military vehicles brought German soldiers—someone must have denounced the scouts. The local Fifth Column kept their eyes open. The scouts were arrested and brought here to this forest. They inhaled the scent of military tarpaulins and the forest floor. As they led them into the forest, one of the boys started running and shots were fired, but he did make it, he escaped. The others got beaten with gun butts. In the clearing, the soldiers asked the boys who had come up with the idea, who had pasted the leaflets on the walls. One of them had the courage to step forward and say that the one who had escaped had done it. The ruse did not work. The Germans lined up the scouts to execute them.

Then another boy started running. He ran off to the side, in between the trees, into a drainage ditch. He frantically dodged the bullets among the trees. They fired shots, but he too made it. After the war, Tadeusz Cieciera gave a witness account of what happened in that clearing. He did not return to Zielonka until 1944, right on time for the Warsaw Uprising.

Those lying in the sand here were the greatest threat to the existence of the Third Reich: Zbigniew Dymek aged 16, Stanisław Golcz aged 16, Józef Wyrzykowski aged 17 . . . these boys were a threat to the biggest and best equipped army in the world, one that was preparing to conquer the world. There are in people, but also in states ruled by madmen—Nero and Caligula, Genghis Khan and Tamerlan, Lenin and Trotsky, Hitler and Mao—unexplored and unfathomable layers of cruelty that must find their outlet every now and then. And back then, those layers of cruelty were found in the Zielonka forest.

Carmen sits. On the grass near the statue, a mother, a daughter, and a father are playing with a ball, which just hit the ground, wildly, scaring the dog. From Carmen's point of view, even a world like this is evil. And from mine? I no longer believe it can be changed. Nothing can be reversed, undone, or forgotten. Nothing of what happened here. Was it a mistake? If so, whose mistake was it?

FOR FREE

"The best gifts are given for free."

— Ernst Jünger, *On the Marble Cliffs*

The bishop's gravestone is in an alley that runs alongside the old cemetery walls. There is a black cross with an engraved inscription. When you stand in front of it, there is a wall behind you, the masons' office and toilets to your right, and a grey church to the left, a short distance away. I never thought that our paths would cross again. To tell you the truth, I had completely forgotten about my bishop. News of his serious illness had reached me several times over the years, but for me this was like any other news, like reports of the Vistula River pollution crisis or of the rail system failure at the Western Station.

I am standing over the bishop's grave now, reciting a prayer for his sake, the first prayer that I have ever recited for him. My wife and our two daughters are standing next to me. The older one, Marysia, is fourteen, and the younger, Zosia, only six. I won't tell them my story about the bishop. I am not so sure I understand it fully myself. Even here, by that black cross to which the deceased remained faithful right until his very end, I won't explain anything, not even to myself, let alone to others, especially young children. All I will say is that this was my former parish priest from the parish of All Saints. Marysia lights a candle with a lighter.

There is a November chill falling on the black cross; that other morning in Grzybowski Square was chilly too. It was past six in the morning, mid-April. I do not know why I am reminded of that day now. Perhaps because I used to think about myself so much at the time—I had feverish thoughts and was full of ideas about Poland's ancient history, about the chronicle writers Gallus Anonymous and Wincenty Kadłubek, about the division of Poland between the deceased king's progeny, and the rebellion of the alderman Albert. What nonsense! It was very interesting, but I was mainly interested in myself, my actions, my future.

In Grzybowski Square, next to the ruined tenement houses on Próżna Street, a carbide firecracker suddenly went off. It made a loud bang, interrupting the flow of my thoughts, and I ducked my head to protect it with my arms, a reflex action like a turtle. Pigeons and crows rushed up from the branches of the black trees overgrowing this space in the middle of a city, a city still under reconstruction.

At that moment, I did not know which direction to take. All the paths crossed senselessly, they seemed to be running nowhere. The April sky, white with streaks of grey, and the Jewish Theatre building with its sandstone slabs, erected on a platform with three concrete steps. I read the show titles: *The Dybbuk and the Maiden, Winter in Anatevka, The Sick Pearls* . . . The theatre was closely associated with the place I knew so well, with the hopelessness of the concrete, the sprouting grass, the piles of black, leftover melting snow in heaps at the kerbs. I knew nothing of the ghetto wall running through the very centre of the square. The All Saints' Church and Próżna Street, which still starts here despite the destruction that took place during the war, were both on the Jewish side.

What I was thinking about at the time, what I knew about the world and about the future in this city, all the fantasies and dreams of a boy who was about to graduate from high school—I put all of these in the mouth of an alabaster statue of Christ, a sculpture by Viktor Brodzki. The Lord Saviour was positioned by the right-hand aisle of the church, the one I kept choosing, and he invariably greeted me with a raised hand. He was full of remarkable solemnity, but also full of grace. He spoke to me quite like he had to the crowds at the Sea of Galilee, whenever I came to the church.

Looking from the nave, in the distance, I sometimes saw this other figure too. Slight, hair kept very short, wearing a black cassock and a white surplice. He would walk towards the confession box and sit in it. Or he would talk quietly to someone under a large pillar that climbed boldly upwards and ended in an arch by the vault. The priest (who later became the bishop) had a quiet and gentle tone of voice. He never raised his voice, even though he talked a lot. He had to, of course, he was our parish priest. I used to listen to his sermons at Sunday Masses, but I don't remember anything he said anymore. During the Midnight Mass on Christmas Eve, he would climb up the wrought-iron, openwork pulpit, so then everyone could see him.

The church, though huge, did not seem too big for either the parish priest or for us. I think it was just right. A Holy Mass in the chapel of Our Lady of Częstochowa on a Friday night. Words from the book of Ezekiel, telling about a valley filled with bones that were very dry. Then with a rattling sound, flesh appears on them and a great army is formed. We sit and listen as he reads to us, which he does without any emphases, with no acting, but rather with simplicity, in a voice that is slightly hushed, the words echoing slightly off the walls of the small chapel. We sit, listening. I would gladly continue listening if I could, but that ended many years ago. The image of the valley remains, which is why I believe that the bishop's body will one day leave the grave by the cemetery wall, the marble slab will crack, and the black cross will lean towards the ground. And there will be a new man, just as in Ezekiel's old vision: "Dry bones, hear the word of the Lord!"

Let us balance this eschatological image with an evocation of the church's cellar. It is spacious and consists of many vaulted rooms and a pleasant coolness lingers there in summer. When it was used as a hospital by the insurgents, people suffered and died on the concrete floors, but at least the chill was their friend. When my parish priest was still there, there was a cinema room where I watched *Amadeus* and movies by Herzog. They made a great impression on me. Then, as I went back home in the dark—the black shape of All Saints' Church to the right, the new buildings on the left, ones that were erected on the rubble of a destroyed city. Through the gate and arcades you could reach Grzybowski Square, then turn left into Twarda Street.

I once met the priest in this passage. It was a warm evening, the pavements were hot from the sun, and the windows in the flats surrounding the square were dimly lit by the glow of black and white television sets. Only the Menorah restaurant, on the ground floor of one of the blocks just off the Bagno Street, was brightly lit.

A dark figure, a cassock, a greeting, a perfunctory conversation. What did we talk about? Two things that have stayed with me to this day, though I did not plan to bring them up. The first was the news programme freshly introduced by the communist TV broadcaster— it was called *Teleexpress*. The news stories flashed one after another at a pace that made our heads spin at the time, and then the presenter with his big-screen smile trying to convince everyone that things were cool in Poland and that we should be happy because salted butter from Denmark and artificial honey were available in the shops.

We talked about *Teleexpress* as a new form of propaganda, then about something else. In the darkness of the church arcade, I could still see his face, his shining eyes, his voice as calm as always, asking that quiet question, casually, returning to some previous thread of conversation:

"Who is Jesus to you? Who is He?"

He left me with it, although for many years I thought I knew the answer, or even many answers, and thus, for many years, the question remained neutral. Everything has been said, read, proven. Witnessed. But the question somehow rattled inside me, along with the black cross on the bishop's grave, two glances and there it is, coming up to the surface, brought with the frothing tidal wave of those years, the memory of Grzybowski Square as it used to be, the times of dirty, decaying communism, those first *Teleexpress* shows.

All that is gone now, long gone. Fortunately, the All Saints' Church is still there, standing in the same place, though the surroundings have changed a lot. Today, the area is dominated by a black obelisk—the Cosmopolitan skyscraper. The Jewish Theatre has been demolished, the vacant plot waiting for the highest bidder. The Menorah restaurant is no longer there either, but other eateries and pubs populate the eastern side of the square, towards Próżna Street. One side of the street has been renovated and spruced up, but the opposite side remains as it was thirty-odd years ago, still decrepit. The corner tenement at no. 14 is particularly depressing, its gate is still guarded by two ferocious cast-iron dwarves.

What else was there back then? What did I see day in and day out in this part of town? Crooked pavements, mud gathering by the kerbs, the steps leading to the church with traces of green lichen, the grey chill of the church porch, the sun-scorched lawn in the middle of the square, the bus stop for line 160 that run towards Targówek. As the bus drove out of the square, the view was towards the block of flats at Graniczna no. 4. The roar of an old Icarus bus, the puff of black exhaust fumes. The moon that sometimes illuminated patches missing in the walls, the stains left by crumbled plaster, a tin dustbin, and a broken bench. Cigarette butts on the concrete pavement.

In the cemetery, there is a grave with a black cross. In the grave lies the bishop, and I stand next to him with my wife and our daughters. Back then, when we talked in the arcades of Grzybowski Square, I did not know that none of my fantasies and the exhortations I made before the alabaster Christ would ever come true. How could I possibly have known that? There is little left of my youthful plans, almost nothing, and I am someone else now. My life has not turned out as I'd imagined it would. Zosia pulls at my sleeve, saying that she is cold. I keep my hands in my pockets, look at the bishop's gravestone, feel the 'Lord's leather' candy with my fingers. Maybe I shall leave it here, offer it to the bishop in gratitude for those years back then?

Postscript: I finished this essay and made a clean copy, then sent it to a Catholic weekly, suggesting they might print it. The anniversary of the bishop's passing was approaching, so I thought perhaps a short piece on the subject would be approved. A few days later, I got a phone call from the editorial secretary, who wished to speak to me about something. The news was unfavourable, and not because the publisher's decision was negative. The reality was much worse. The protagonist of my story was proven to be a secret collaborator of the communist Security Service—there were papers, there were files. The weekly decided not to publish my essay because it would show only part of the truth about him. "Had you known about this, you would probably have written your story in a different way," the secretary said. Perhaps. Still, my recollections of those times are as I have recorded them here. They are true and new knowledge will not change them. However, I decided to complete the text by adding this new and very unpleasant piece of information. The bishop wrote reports, denounced others, had meetings with his assigned officer. Did he harm anyone? I am writing about this because I think I have the right to demand that the full truth about a man I once trusted be revealed. What would literature become without truth? A lie. It is not very likely that someone else will write about it, so that is why I am doing it. My protagonist was not a character akin to the one in the opening passages of *Les Miserables* by Victor Hugo, the bishop who helped Jean Valjean at a crucial moment in his life. He was someone else. May he rest in peace.

CHRISTMAS EVE IN A GARAGE

Poldek liked boiled cabbage, lightly stewed with mushrooms. It was the best! Sweet and filling, a large portion was steaming on the plate, along with a slice of bread bought at the bakery on Staszica Street. It was the Christmas season. Czesia had cooked the cabbage—one just had to taste it before serving it to guests at Christmas dinner. A shot of vodka would go nicely with the cabbage, but his wife and his daughter made sure Poldek stayed healthy and did nothing stupid. Retirement. Heart issues. Coronary. He used to like moonshine very much and had been making it for years, but he has passed his equipment on to Hipek. If he was younger, he could still use it well. The still consisted of a steel milk can in which the mash fermented, a spiralling tube, and a bucket with an attached faucet for the 'raw material drain,' as Poldek used to say on nights when his liquor production was in full swing.

The cabbage always smelled wonderful. It was hot, steam rising from the plate along with the smell, which by now had permeated the whole house. The smell of cabbage means safety—it marks the boundary of what is familiar and friendly. Poldek makes his brew, Lipton, his favorite. It has a good, strong taste. He used to take a shot of Monopolka or moonshine as an essential digestive medication. Good for your health! And today? Tea, television—the next episode of the Polish series *The Crown of the Kings* is about to start. Oh, the plate is empty. How about a refill? He takes a sneak peek into the pot. Okay, just another spoon and a half. At least it is not meat. In his family, everyone always favoured cabbage, ever since they were little—his mother, his father, and siblings. And they were quite a few of them. To list them by birth: Heniek, Marian, Poldek, Marynia, Czesiek, Miecia, Helcia, Ania, and Józek. In the villages, cabbage was shredded in autumn and put into a barrel. The barrel was made of wood, the staves tightened with hoops made of iron tape, then you had to roll the barrel to the cellar in the backyard.

And there was no mess in the courtyard. Chickens, yes, and that meant that when it rained, it was messy, but otherwise very tidy. His father made sure it stayed that way. There were no boards or chopped firewood lying about, let alone old buckets or rusty pots and plough parts. Nothing of the sort. In the springtime or in the summer, they always swept the yard clean with a wicker broom. Their father was particular about tidiness, made sure they kept things orderly, because he was a true farmer.

Czesia is sitting opposite Poldek. In front of her, there is another deep plate from which she eats her cabbage. This is the best way to eat cabbage—there is always a bit of the sweet sauce left at the bottom of the plate and you can dip a slice of bread in it. The plates are beige with a print of blue and red flowers, and the spoons are aluminum, the best kind, because they are light. All of this has been arranged on the kitchen table which is covered with a tablecloth with a brown and beige pattern. Their meal now finished—late lunch or early dinner, it does not matter as long as the cabbage is in the pot, you can satisfy your hunger at any time of the day. All you have to do is reheat the pot.

Soon, the next episode of another series will be on. Czesia knows the whole TV programme by heart—she won't miss any new episodes. They say that in the past there was nothing to watch on telly, just two channels, whereas now we have ten, but Poldek has fond memories of *Return to Eden, Escrava Isaura,* and *Oshin,* which was about a young Japanese girl from a poor village, and *Die Schwarzwaldklinik.* These were good shows. The new ones have better colours because technology has advanced, but they are not more interesting than the old ones. And there was the Polish costume drama *Nights and Days*—a beautiful series—ladies in elegant gowns, carriages. Poldek and Czesia liked it, and even now, whenever there is a rerun, they watch it with pleasure. At different times, different things moved them. When they were younger, they had more energy and were smarter. Now that they are retired, it is not bad either— there is nothing to complain about. They cannot complain.

Czesia takes their plates. She sees that Poldek won't eat any more. She knows him like the back of her hand. Or like both the palm and the back? She moves towards the sink, her hunched back now clearly visible. She has rickets, something Hipek has joked about over the years. Poldek should have told him off in front of the whole family for it, but in the end he never did. And he gave Hipek his moonshine production equipment because he had no one else to give it to. Jacuś only drinks Monopolka, and his grandchildren, Krzysio and Tomuś, do not seem to drink at all, which is good. Every generation should drink less vodka than the older one, that was Poldek's thinking. In any case, things were moving in a new direction, and at his granddaughter Basia's wedding there were fewer people drinking than before; it was all very cultured with a gurgling fountain in the middle of the room and everyone having a good time, no one needed to be escorted out because they were practising karate strokes like Józek, Poldek's late younger brother who drank himself to death, once did. Different times, but Poldek suspects that maybe people drink less because there are more drugs. Who knows? In any case, less vodka is being consumed in Poland now. It is a notable fact.

The cabbage dish is filling, heavy, and Poldek is overwhelmed by blissful laziness. If it weren't for *The Crown of the Kings*, he would have taken a nap in the other room. He has to be careful not to fall asleep during the episode! Their kitchen has light birchwood panelling, which has been there for many years, though the wood has not darkened at all. The picture of Our Lady of Częstochowa hangs above the table, glued onto a wood panel and varnished to a shine. Below it is a shelf with a plastic saltshaker and a mushroom-shaped nutcracker. There is a dip in one end of the handle where the threaded pin goes in as you tighten it, and the nut gets crushed. A gift from Hipek. What else? Everything a kitchen should have, plus a gift from Luisa—a modern mixer, displayed in the cabinet near the sink. Poldek does not touch it at all. Maybe it is not a mixer but a kitchen robot, that is what Czesia keeps saying—who the fuck knows what it is. It is there, and sometimes it makes a lot of noise, and then Poldek just leaves the kitchen because it is unbearable. They make this weird stuff nowadays to rip people off.

The TV show will start soon. Czesia paces around the room, and switches the Christmas tree lights on. At the very top of the tree, there is a star. The TV is on, with all the ads. Come on! Poldek settles down in his armchair, the cabbage in his belly nice and warm, King Casimir the Great on the telly settling his love affairs. That man had stamina! He chased them all, pursued all of his countless opportunities—what woman would say no to a king? It was an honour to have him do it to her. And now the king wants to sleep with a Jewish girl, Polish girls are not enough for him. She is so pretty! Dark! Czesia also likes Esterka—she expresses her approval with a series of silent gasps. He is so horny, that fucker! And you can see that she has her dignity. She comes from a rich family and is a decent girl. Not like all those tarts at a disco. When there is a party in Nowa Wieś, the bushes never stop shaking. At least that is what the village leader told him when they were standing in front of the shop, reinforcing themselves with a beer. It is supposed to be a decent village, but when people come to the village party by car—and nowadays every kid has a car—they go into the forest. So many condoms lying around in the grass there, can you imagine? But even condoms won't do the trick, and the girls then parade their big bellies around the village. So shameless! They want to have it all now! The village leader took a big swig and looked at the roof of the cottage on the other side of the village road. The last thatched roof in the village. The stork built its nest there.

Poldek and Czesia used to go to Nowa Wieś to pick mushrooms. It was his home village and he knew every fieldstone there. When their timing was right, they would bring home a bucket full of penny buns, sometimes more. They had a fierce mushroom competition with Hipek. That one really knew a thing or two about mushrooms. Strangely enough, he always came to pick them on the same days as Poldek. He was so clever that he could spot them both in meadows and by the fields. He would lay them all out on a chopping board and call Poldek to come and have a look at his harvest. In any case, there will be plenty of mushrooms this winter. They have already eaten so many of them, including today in their cabbage. They've eaten them stewed in a pan with chopped onions, topped on a pork chop, and with boiled potatoes with butter and fresh, chopped dill. That is a real meal, not like those pizzas and kebabs, his grandchildren's favourite treats. Grandpa, grandpa, give me some money so I can order pizza!

Casimir the Great is a fierce competitor, too! He has already had his way with Esther. They lay in a bed with a canopy in a high vaulted chamber. All his wishes granted. And on top of that, he became a great king. Go figure.

There is a knock on the door.

"Who the hell is that?" Poldek grumbles as he gets up.

It is Hipek.

"Come in, brother. It is the end of *The Crown of the Kings* episode, aren't you watching?"

"Greetings my lady," Hipek says to Czesia, but she only nods at him, her gaze fixed on the royal amorous exploits, the final minutes, and the preview of tomorrow's episode.

Hipek politely sits in his chair and stares at the screen. Poldek immediately sees what he has in his pocket. Will Czesia notice? Because if she does, there will be a buzz. So, when the end credits roll, Poldek quickly says:

"Hipek, come on, let's go to the garage, I have prepared the boiler and the can for you, so you can have a look."

"Do you want some cabbage?" Czesia asks, but Hipek thanks her and says that he has already eaten.

"We may reheat it later." Poldek opens the door to the vestibule and turns on the light to the stairs leading down to the cellar and the garage.

On their way, they pass by bags of old shoes, empty bottles and jars, a sack of onions, a bucket of potatoes, and a basket full of rags, all stored on the steps. Poldek was supposed to carry it all down to the cellar, but somehow he had other things to do. He and Czesia have already fought about it a few times.

The ceiling is low and they need to bend their heads. Hipek does it instinctively—he is at home here. In the first room there are heaters—an old, coal-fired one that they have been using since the house was built, and next to it, a gas one. The gas one was installed a few years ago, but it keeps breaking down, rattling. Poldek has called in a specialist again, but these guys take their time. They come when they happen to have free time and there is no better-paying job. The repairman was supposed to pop in last week but did not and hasn't even called.

Now they are in the woodshed. Firewood was brought in from Nowa Wieś and stacked evenly against the walls with a farmer's hand—you can see it. Once in a while, Poldek's son and daughter-in-law take a few logs for their fireplace.

"Look, I bought a tonne of coal since I don't know if I'll be able to run my gas stove in the winter."

And there is another cellar room. This is where they store potatoes, onions, and beetroot—all the vegetables lie in sacks—from the farmers in Nowa Wieś. There is also the old furniture from Luisa's room—a desk, a table, and four chairs. She bought herself new things a long time ago, but since these are still in good condition, Poldek keeps them because maybe they will come in handy or someone will need them. Too much is not a problem.

They reach the garage and Poldek turns on the light. The pungent smell of oil paint which he recently used to paint the fence posts and squares. Some is still left in a large tin. Near the car, under the tiny window, there is an old desk with a vise bolted on, tools, nails in jars and tin boxes, screws, nuts in paper candy boxes. The tabletop is black with grease, nicked and split. Next to it, dusty electrical wires and tools hang from the wall, plastic bags in which Poldek stores spare parts for his car.

Now he takes one of the cords and plugs it into a socket. A small Christmas tree starts to twinkle on the desk.

"Nice, eh?"

"Sure is! Where did you get it?"

"Jacek's kids wanted to throw it away, and I have a use for it."

Near a wooden box without a lid, in which he keeps his files and screwdrivers, there are two clean vodka glasses. Poldek reaches behind the desk, fiddles there for a while and takes out a jar of pickled plums in vinegar, his favourite.

"Czesia won't be griping?" Hipek asks, just for the record, as he takes out a "1906" bottle of vodka, "commonly known as vintage," from his inside pocket.

"She will complain and then she will stop, it is holiday time."

The lights keep flashing. The two men sit on stools and Poldek pours them a drink. They drink. The jar of pickled plums is difficult to open, but finally the lid pops off with a quiet clack. The host hands Hipek a plum he has fished out with a fork.

Hipek removes it from the fork with his fingers and pushes it into his mouth. He chews. They fall silent for a while. Poldek pours out another shot. Drink up! The pace slows. They are no longer young and cannot have a shot every five minutes or so. Youth coupled with stamina. Maybe that is why Hipek says:

"Used to be a beer stall at the Eastern Station. We used to go there after work and always spiked the beer with a shot of vodka. It was so good!"

"Do you want some beer?"

Poldek opens the desk cupboard and takes out a can of Harnaś beer. He puts it on the counter, right next to the flask. Then he says:

"Hipek, look, what's with these Jews—Casimir the Great fell in love with a Jewish woman, and we used to have a Jewish woman hiding in a cowshed with her children."

"During the war?"

Poldek is silent and pretends to study the bonnet of his twenty-year-old cream-coloured Ford Fiesta. Not a trace of rust on the bodywork after all these years.

"I was small. How old was I? About eight. Once our father was milking the cow in the morning and I said to him: 'Dad, Dad, someone's walking in the yard,' and he told me: 'Poldek, there's no one there.' He didn't want us to know . . ."

"Sure, if the kids find out, all the village will know."

Another moment of silence.

"Shall we? Hipek, pour us a drink, for I am getting a bit sad."

They drink. Another plum in vinegar, sweet, but not too sweet, and sour, but not too sour. Hipek shakes his shaggy head, already peppered with streaks of grey. He has known Poldek for years, but he never heard about the cowshed until now.

"There was a whole family there: the Jew, the pregnant woman, and three children. They were hiding upstairs, and our father and mother knew all about it, but we kids did not. Then my mother told me everything: at night the Jew would come down from the attic and go around the village looking for food. One morning he came to my father's barn because he wanted milk for the children. A neighbour called out, saying the Germans were in the village. The Jew got scared and started to run towards the forest, because our cottage was closest to it, you remember how it was, but they saw him and started shooting, but he managed to run away."

"And the others?"

"There was much screaming, crying, wailing. The pregnant woman despaired because she thought they had killed her husband. Then one of the Germans climbed into the attic using a potato planting rod and saw them—the Jews that were there. And he asked my mother: "'Where is your husband?' My father was in the field and they sent me to bring him. They started the interrogation right away. My father denied it all, saying that he didn't know anything, that he had never seen anyone, that he only found out today that they were hiding in there."

"They were in his own house and he did not know!" Hipek huffed.

"My father knew, and my mother knew, it is clear as the sun in the sky," Poldek confirmed and then continued:

"The German commander decided that all the Jews should be shot dead. They had already taken my father and the Jewish woman and the children out. But, apparently, they decided they wanted to check whether the Poles were lying. And do you know how?"

"Did they bother to do that? Shall we have another shot?"

They drank and snacked. The day slowly came to an end, but it got merrier in the garage. The lights on the Christmas tree twinkled colourfully, reflected in the half-empty bottle. Even the grey light seeping in through the dusty garage window did not spoil the festive mood. Another bonus was the familiar smell of oil, petrol, wood, and old rags. Shadows travelled on the wall next to onion crates and plastic bags of crushed beer cans.

"That same day, my mother saw through the window that some-one was climbing into the barn using the same rod. She jumped out of the house and saw some guy. She ran to him and shouted: 'Get out of here, Jew, don't you know the Germans took my husband, get out of here!' She has a go at him and tugs on his trousers. Then the guy gets down and shows her that under the coat he is wearing the German military uniform. You get that? They wanted to check whether my mother was really hiding Jews or not."

"She was a simple woman. She didn't finish any school," Hipek joins in.

Poldek nods.

"And my father came back home that evening."

"And what about the Jews?"

"The Germans demanded carts and took the wife and children away, and the man who ran away was never heard of again. Did he make it? Did he not make it?"

"There is no way to find out," Hipek concludes, already speaking gibberish.

Poldek reaches for his glass and pushes his fingers into the jar of plums. He is visibly drunk.

"Can you imagine—a simple woman."

They drink the last shot before they part. Poldek hides the empty flask in the desk and opens the beer.

"And Czesia won't be angry?"

Abracadabra: there is a small glass in Poldek's hand. He pours the golden liquid up to the rim and hands the glass to Hipek.

BUT YOU ARE A MERE MORTAL

There is a very strong painkiller sold over the counter and advertised on TV. People will get it all mixed up—you see, they will think it is the same as other medicines with milder effects, like panadol, ibuprom—and after taking ketoprofen many people have experienced problems—dizziness, even fainting. Not to mention damage to their liver or intestines. You can even die if you take it when you have certain underlying conditions. You have some pain in your arm for a few days, so you buy a medication at the pharmacy, you swallow a pill while sitting and watching the telly, and you die. All because you've had some pain in your arm for a few days.

And what do you say about her? She is beautiful, isn't she? Big dark eyes, dark hair, slim. Full lips. Okay, I agree, she may not be an outstanding beauty, but I am happy with what I got. She serves me quickly, and when I ask for a spoon to stir my Turkish coffee, she brings it but informs me that such coffee does not need to be stirred at all. She is cheeky. Surely you would have continued the repartee, but I remain silent. I overhear her conversation with the bartender. He is wearing a T-shirt with an inscription in the reformed Cyrillic script that says: "Independent." I don't associate Ukrainian speech with anything in particular—it just is, like this girl's body in her black waitress outfit: a blouse showing cleavage and tight trousers that emphasise her buttocks.

It's stuffy in the office today. The fan is just stirring the air, and I get a headache from its muffled hum. Ketoprofen? Outside the window there is a neglected courtyard, like many others in Warsaw.

If I were to describe it to you: on one side, you have garages under locks, with sheets of plaster and pieces of brick falling on their roofs from the top of the tenement building. Grass has sprouted in the gutters. On the opposite side, looking out from my window, there are annexes and extensions, painted yellow. There used to be small shops, service outlets, but they have been shut for many years. Signboards have survived: 'Tao Universe' and 'Dog Grooming.' The tar paper-covered roof has holes in it. Pigeons enter the largest hole and nest there. There are two chimneys sticking out of the roof, decaying along with it.

Lots of pigeons in this yard—their carcasses can often be found sprawled on the tarmac with tyre tracks imprinted on them. The dead birds are food for crows, and perhaps pigeons also peck on each other. On the left, right next to my window, there is another extension attached to the wall of the neighbouring building. Above the entrance, a concrete canopy overgrown with moss, blinded windows, bars, plywood, and a small birch tree that has sprouted there shakes on the roof of this ruin. Pity you can't see it, it's so graceful! In front of the entrance that has now been closed for years there is a sign: 'Silver Plating.' And there are cars parked in the courtyard: a black Mercedes, a green Range Rover, and a white Toyota. Apart from that, there is nothing going on. Oh, and there is a broken office chair. I see it every day and often wonder who used to spin on it.

The railing on the bus is cool and smooth. The little girl's eyes stare at me and, just behind her, behind the plexiglass, other eyes, huge eyes, even bigger than those of the Ukrainian waitress, also stare at me. Oh, the full alertness to life, a woman, or perhaps life itself, invincible, it holds us by the throat every day, even here, on the 116 bus line.

Can you hear it? Listen to this: "Because you think you are wise, as wise as a god, I am going to bring foreigners against you, the most ruthless of nations; they will draw their swords against your beauty and wisdom and pierce your shining splendor. They will bring you down to the pit, and you will die a violent death in the heart of the seas. Will you then say, 'I am a god,' in the presence of those who kill you?"

A woman stands alone in a pew. When the priest says your name, she is the only one who wipes her tears away. Apart from her, no one here is crying for you, no one is moved at this particular moment. The bright dome covers us now. There is the late afternoon light of one of the last days of summer. Life has come full circle. August has been very hot this year. Girls all over Warsaw barely wear any clothes, even girls who would normally never wear skimpy dresses, shorts, or expose their thighs and arms had to this summer. The festival is still going on—it's a shame you cannot watch.

The priest lifts the host. We kneel, and an oblique sunbeam hits the open cut on the side of Christ, there on the cross. A crucifix of white wood, new workmanship—you can see it is solid carpentry. Then just another while and there comes the blessing. Outside the church, your mother approaches a group of people, she thinks they knew you from somewhere, she probably wants to thank them. They shake their heads. I quickly say hello to her.

The path between the blocks of flats is winding, and if it wasn't for your mother, I would be lost here for sure. We talk about you— who else could we talk about. The only thing we have in common is memories, so we reminisce about the time you drunkenly threw the remote control out of the window and threatened to do the same to your mother. And so many other stories. The evening is very warm and we sit on a bench in front of your block, picture after picture flies by, you're in every one of them. It means a lot to me. I feel grateful. A guy wearing sandals walks past us and bows to your mother. A neighbour. You probably knew him when you were alive, didn't you?

The tarmac alley goes on forever. A child on a bicycle rides towards me, followed by Agnieszka, a friend of mine. We used to go to primary school together. I haven't seen her for twenty years or more. Still we recognize each other. Her little girl has gone too far away and Agnieszka has to chase after her, so we say goodbye.

"Take care, all the best."

In just a few seconds, will there be another meeting like this? Maybe not. On the left, a huge playground, lots of children. This is where my friend and her daughter were coming from. Life goes on, teeming among the blocks of flats in Stegny. The day is coming to an end. For me, it has flown by as quickly as the last year, since you decided to part with your mother and the world.

THE RIVER

Slow flowing, wide, cold and clear water. Shallow—in summer even a child can cross it safely and reach the other bank. You only need to wear sandals as the entire riverbed is lined with pebbles. The current makes the stones slippery with vegetation and small creatures feed on it, hiding under the stone as soon as there is the slightest disturbance in the water surface. These insects are not, thank God, poisonous, they are completely benign and very skittish. Their rapid movement shows that there is life on the surface of the stones.

One day I picked up such a stone from the bottom of the river and turned it over, wanting to see a tiny fleeing creature, but there was only a bit of fragrant silt. Its dark vegetal green stuck to my fingers.

I used to bathe here in the summer. The water was shallow, deeper in one place only, which we called 'under the rock.' It was a big rock on the bank opposite the town beach. It went sharply upwards and was overgrown with mixed forest. The water was always cool as it flowed from the mountains. Therefore, on hot days, it was best to take a dip in it straight away. How pleasant!

I even managed to dive under the rock with a snorkelling mask on because I was very small. Suddenly, I found myself surrounded by silence and fish mouths sticking out from the crevices between the rocks. I reached out my hand and they disappeared. I kept swimming—I mean clinging to the stones, scraping my belly on the slippery riverbed. It was a nice feeling, the mossy stones were very soft, but I had to go back to the surface, already out of breath.

Above the water, the sunshine, forming scale patterns on the water, coming from the side of the railway bridge, blinding. I have to squint. I turn my head. In the distance, you can see a second bridge painted blue and its railings are two-tone, blue and white. Lorries, cars, local buses pass over it, but you can't see them from here.

The smell of the river water. The stones on both banks, hot after the heat of the day, also belong to the river; in the sunlight these pebbles appear to be white and seem to be arranged side by side. Who has arranged them like this? What force? A human being would certainly not have devised this pattern, so soothing to the eye the more one gazes at it. There is a hidden movement of water in these stones, the water that brought them here and continued on, indifferently, towards the Vistula, where this river ends its course.

That day Oczkowska dipped her swollen feet into the perfectly cold water. A feeling incomparable to any other. She was on her way to Maków, had walked through Germany and the whole of Silesia, then took a train from Bielsko-Biała to Kraków, travelling on foot again and sleeping in good people's barns, fearful of the Soviet soldiers with the red star on their caps who would always have their way with a woman, young or old. The skin on her feet was rubbed raw, her toes twisted from wearing the camp clogs. When she reached the town, she turned right, towards the wooden bridge that went down to the riverbank.

The Skawa rolled on. It had not gotten much bigger that spring. The vegetation on the bank was already lush. The girl pushed away the tall stalks of wild dill with both her hands. She made her way through the burdock bushes growing on the patches of earth between the stones. Nothing else grew after that. Oczkowska laid her bundle on the stones; in it, she had half a loaf of bread, a knife, a spare shawl to cover her head and shoulders, a tortoiseshell comb, a piece of hard soap wrapped in a cloth, and a bottle to fill with water. She took off her striped suit and carefully placed it next to the bundle. Her lean, pale arms absorbed the green flowing of the river. She sat down on a larger stone, took off her shapeless boots, and unwound her blood-stained foot wraps.

Cold. She kept her feet in the water for a long time, and when she looked up at the sky a few moments later, she saw a kestrel circling. Then a shot was fired in the distance, but she did not even bother to turn her head. The surrounding mountains reverberated with an echo that faded somewhere further down the ravine. Wet stones and the smell of silt. A branch moved and a large bird fluttered in the crown of a tree on the other side of the river. At Ravensbrück, shots were fired every day, so she was used to it. During the first months in the camp, she was overwhelmed with fear—a shot, then a burst of automatic gunfire would paralyse her in the barracks and at work when she pushed a wheelbarrow filled with stones up a high embankment. Afterwards, she was no longer afraid of gunshots, only of being taken to the wall where they executed women prisoners.

Can you imagine that when all of that was happening, the Skawa kept running its same course with a gentle murmuring? That here and there islands made of pebbles emerged from its current, and dry boughs entwined with duckweed, and in the river's meandering curve, under the overhanging branches of large trees, the pond skaters flashed in and out? Probably not, it was a different world, but Oczkowska was now back with herself, back with the river. She was still young, and she felt she was recovering her former life more and more with every passing moment.

I persevered and swam in the Skawa River. Then it was lunch-time, followed by a lazy afternoon, which I spent wandering around the town and the neighbouring area. At the cinema, they screened films every day. I had seen all parts of the East German Winnetou and Old Shatterhand saga. I shared the excitement with my grandmother, as she peeled potatoes over the bucket. Then I gazed up at the sky above the red-tiled barn, where frayed clouds floated gently.

"Granny, why does Mrs. Oczkowska have such crooked toes?"

"It is because of the camp clogs."

"Granny, why does she crumble bread into a plate of milk and only then eat it?"

"Because she has no teeth."

"Granny . . ."

"Come on, give me a break, pestering me with all these questions."

The next day the cold water glistened in the sun again. An inexhaustible source of coolness and comfort. The surrounding mountains watched the river flowing patiently. To come here and immerse yourself in the green water must be like forgetting everything, even if only for a moment.

ACKNOWLEDGEMENTS

Thank you to Joseph Pearce, and to the team at Wiseblood Books including Joshua Hren, Mary R. Finnegan, Janille Stephens, and Kathy West. Special thanks to Jan J. Franczak. This publication has been supported by the ©POLAND Translation Program.

The stories published in the present edition first appeared in the following books and journals:

Brzytwa (2008): The Roma Woman; The Village Beneath the Sand; Roman and the Girl

Najlepsza dentystka w Londynie (2014): A Prayer; Gertrud von le Fort; Deventer; St Joseph Freinademetz

Magiczne światło miasta (2019): When it rains; Dog Food

Sylwia z Gibalaka i inne opowiadania (2023): The Chłodna Street Fantasy; Repeated Mistakes; For Free; But You Are a Mere Mortal

Tygodnik TVP # 109, 20.12.2019: Christmas Eve in a Garage [online]

Tygodnik TVP # 285, 5.05.2023: White Week [online]

Twórczość 2023, issue 3 (928): The River.

WORKS CITED

Strahlungen by Ernst Jünger, published as *A German Officer in Occupied Paris: The War Journals, 1941–1945*, translated by Thomas S. Hansen and Abby J. Hansen.

The Holy Bible, New International Version published by Biblica.

The Charge of the Light Brigade by Alfred, Lord Tennyson.

Through the Eyes of a Child. Recollections from Childhood Spent in the Ghetto and Concentration Camps by Stella Müller-Madej.

Faust by Johann Wolfgang von Goethe, translated by Bayard Taylor.

Prayer by Wen Yiduo, translated by Robert Hammond Dorsett.

Mistakes by Stefan Żeromski.

On the Marble Cliffs by Ernst Jünger, translated by Tess Lewis.

The Rings of Saturn by W.G. Sebald, translated by Michael Hulse.

ABOUT THE AUTHOR

Wojciech Chmielewski (b. 1969) is a fiction writer, essayist, literary critic and playwright for the Polish Radio Theatre. He is best known for his short stories associated with Warsaw. He received the Cyprian Kamil Norwid Literary Award for his novel *Belweder gryzie w rękę* (*Belweder Bites the Hand*, 2018) and was the first winner of the Marek Nowakowski Literary Award for short-story writers (2017), granted as a general recognition for the author's entire body of work.

ABOUT THE TRANSLATOR

Katarzyna Byłów is a translator of Polish, English, and French literature, and is a member of the Polish Association of Literary Translators. She holds a PhD from the University of St. Andrews in Scotland, and as a social anthropologist by training and a literary translator by vocation, she firmly believes in dialogue fostered by literature.